Erle Stanley Gardner and The Murder Room

>>> This title is part of The Murder Room, our series dedicated to making available out-of-print or hard-to-find titles by classic crime writers.

Crime fiction has always held up a mirror to society. The Victorians were fascinated by sensational murder and the emerging science of detection; now we are obsessed with the forensic detail of violent death. And no other genre has so captivated and enthralled readers.

Vast troves of classic crime writing have for a long time been unavailable to all but the most dedicated frequenters of second-hand bookshops. The advent of digital publishing means that we are now able to bring you the backlists of a huge range of titles by classic and contemporary crime writers, some of which have been out of print for decades.

From the genteel amateur private eyes of the Golden Age and the femmes fatales of pulp fiction, to the morally ambiguous hard-boiled detectives of mid twentieth-century America and their descendants who walk our twenty-first century streets, The Murder Room has it all. >>>

The Murder Room
Where Criminal Minds Meet

themurderroom.com

Erle Stanley Gardner (1889–1970)

Born in Malden, Massachusetts, Erle Stanley Gardner left school in 1909 and attended Valparaiso University School of Law in Indiana for just one month before he was suspended for focusing more on his hobby of boxing that his academic studies. Soon after, he settled in California, where he taught himself the law and passed the state bar exam in 1911. The practise of law never held much interest for him, however, apart from as it pertained to trial strategy, and in his spare time he began to write for the pulp magazines that gave Dashiell Hammett and Raymond Chandler their start. Not long after the publication of his first novel, *The Case of the Velvet Claws*, featuring Perry Mason, he gave up his legal practice to write full time. He had one daughter, Grace, with his first wife, Natalie, from whom he later separated. In 1968 Gardner married his long-term secretary, Agnes Jean Bethell, whom he professed to be the real 'Della Street', Perry Mason's sole (although unacknowledged) love interest. He was one of the most successful authors of all time and at the time of his death, in Temecula, California in 1970, is said to have had 135 million copies of his books in print in America alone.

By *Erle Stanley Gardner*
(titles below include only those
published in the Murder Room)

Perry Mason series

The Case of the Sulky Girl
  (1933)
The Case of the Baited Hook
  (1940)
The Case of the Borrowed
  Brunette (1946)
The Case of the Lonely Heiress
  (1948)
The Case of the Negligent
  Nymph (1950)
The Case of the Moth-Eaten
  Mink (1952)
The Case of the Glamorous
  Ghost (1955)
The Case of the Terrified
  Typist (1956)
The Case of the Gilded Lily
  (1956)
The Case of the Lucky Loser
  (1957)
The Case of the Long-Legged
  Models (1958)
The Case of the Deadly Toy
  (1959)
The Case of the Singing Skirt
  (1959)

The Case of the Duplicate
  Daughter (1960)
The Case of the Blonde
  Bonanza (1962)

Cool and Lam series

The Bigger They Come (1939)
Turn on the Heat (1940)
Gold Comes in Bricks (1940)
Spill the Jackpot (1941)
Double or Quits (1941)
Owls Don't Blink (1942)
Bats Fly at Dusk (1942)
Cats Prowl at Night (1943)
Crows Can't Count (1946)
Fools Die on Friday (1947)
Bedrooms Have Windows
  (1949)
Some Women Won't Wait (1953)
Beware the Curves (1956)
You Can Die Laughing (1957)
Some Slips Don't Show (1957)
The Count of Nine (1958)
Pass the Gravy (1959)
Kept Women Can't Quit (1960)
Bachelors Get Lonely (1961)
Shills Can't Count Chips (1961)

Try Anything Once (1962)
Fish or Cut Bait (1963)
Up For Grabs (1964)
Cut Thin to Win (1965)
Widows Wear Weeds (1966)
Traps Need Fresh Bait (1967)

Doug Selby D.A. series

The D.A. Calls it Murder (1937)
The D.A. Holds a Candle (1938)
The D.A. Draws a Circle (1939)
The D.A. Goes to Trial (1940)
The D.A. Cooks a Goose (1942)
The D.A. Calls a Turn (1944)
The D.A. Takes a Chance (1946)
The D.A. Breaks an Egg (1949)

Terry Clane series

Murder Up My Sleeve (1937)
The Case of the Backward
  Mule (1946)

Gramp Wiggins series

The Case of the Turning Tide
  (1941)
The Case of the Smoking
  Chimney (1943)

Two Clues (two novellas) (1947)

Owls Don't Blink

Erle Stanley Gardner

An Orion book

Copyright © The Erle Stanley Gardner Trust 1956

The right of Erle Stanley Gardner to be identified as the author of this work has been asserted in accordance with the Copyright, Designs and Patents Act 1988.

This edition published by
The Orion Publishing Group Ltd
Orion House
5 Upper St Martin's Lane
London WC2H 9EA

An Hachette UK company
A CIP catalogue record for this book is available from the British Library

ISBN 978 1 4719 0886 6

www.orionbooks.co.uk

CHAPTER ONE

I WAS AWAKENED at three o'clock in the morning by the sound of a garbage-pail cover being kicked across the sidewalk. A moment later, a woman's voice, harsh and shrill, shouted, "I am *not* going with you! *Do you understand?*"

I rolled over and tried to drop back into the oblivion of slumber. The woman's voice pursued me, tearing at my eardrums. I couldn't hear the man with whom she was arguing.

The air was heavy with humidity. The bed was a big four-poster antique, placed in the back of a high-ceilinged bedroom. Huge French windows opened onto a balcony, lined with wrought-iron grillwork. This balcony extended out over the sidewalk. Directly across the narrow street was Jack O'Leary's Bar.

When I had tried closing the windows, the heavy, muggy air had made the room stifling. When I opened the big windows, sounds from the old French Quarter of New Orleans came pouring in.

The screaming voice ceased abruptly, and I started drifting off once more into slumber.

Then a fresh disturbance broke out. Someone started playing little tunes on an automobile horn. After a little while, another horn chimed in.

I got up, kicked my feet into slippers, and walking over to the open window, looked across at Jack O'Leary's Bar.

Apparently some roisterer had gone out to get the car and driven down to pick up the rest of his party. He leaned on the horn with a long blast, then a succession

1

of short blasts to let his companions—and the world at large—know he was there. While he blocked the street, another motorist wanted to get by. Other cars rolled up. Soon the whole street was echoing to the din of repeated clamor. As the pressure behind the motorist who was blocking the road became more insistent, he tried to get action out of his own party by pressing the palm of his hand against the horn button and holding it there.

It was a one-way street, with parking permitted on both sides, leaving only a narrow lane down the center for the traffic. The congestion stretched back for a block now. The clamor was insistent, terrific.

Three people came straggling out from Jack O'Leary's Bar: a tall, loose-jointed man in evening clothes who seemed to be in no particular hurry, two girls with long gowns trailing the sidewalk, both of them talking at once, looking back over their shoulders into the lighted bar.

The man waved his hand at the driver of the automobile. The horns pulsed into a cacophony.

The man walked leisurely across the sidewalk, stepped out into the street, and gallantly stood by the rear door, holding it open. After a few seconds, one of the women came over to join him. The other one turned back toward the bar. A fat man in a business suit, holding a glass in his hand, came out to talk with her.

The two people who were holding up the procession seemed completely oblivious of it all. They talked earnestly. The man pulled out a pencil, fished a notebook from his pocket, then looked around for a place to set the glass. When he could find none, he tried to hold glass and notebook in one hand while he scribbled.

Eventually it was completed. The young woman pulled up her long skirt, strolled leisurely across the sidewalk to the curb, and got into the car.

Then followed the slamming of car doors. The driver of the automobile seemed to feel that he could best minimize the delay he had caused by starting in low gear with the throttle wide open. He clashed into second gear at the corner. The stream of congested traffic started flowing by.

I looked at my wrist watch. Three-forty-five.

I stood by the window for half an hour because there was nothing else to do. I couldn't go back to sleep. Bertha Cool was due to arrive on the 7:20 train. I'd told her I'd be at the station to meet her.

During the half hour that I stood, watching the breaking-up of the parties over at O'Leary's Bar, I got so I could just about classify the potential disturbances before they exploded into noise.

There was the battling foursome that would stand out in front and argue at the top of their voices where they should go next. These usually divided into two people who wanted to go home, and two who insisted that it was just the beginning of the evening. There were the people who had made new acquaintances at the bar. Apparently it never occurred to anyone to try and get names, addresses, and telephone numbers until they reached the sidewalk. There the defect was remedied with much laughter, shouted farewells, and some last bit of repartee which could only be remembered when the parties were almost out of earshot. There were the parties-breaking-up-in-a-brawl type of thing—the women who *wouldn't* be seduced—the wives who weren't going to go home *yet*.

Quite evidently it was noisy inside the bar. People emerging to stand on the sidewalk stood close and shouted at each other.

Following the New Orleans custom in the French Quarter, garbage pails were placed on the sidewalks near the curb. Everyone felt it was the height of wit to kick the covers off the garbage pails and listen to them make noise as they slid along the sidewalk.

After half an hour, I crossed over to a chair, sat down, and let my eyes drift around the half-illuminated apartment. Roberta Fenn had lived in this same apartment some three years ago, which would have been 1939. She had rented it under an assumed name; then she had disappeared into thin air. *Cool and Lam—Confidential Investigations* had been hired to find her.

Sitting there in the warm darkness, I tried to reconstruct the life Roberta Fenn must have lived. She must have heard the same sounds I was hearing. She must have eaten at the near-by restaurants, had drinks at the bars, perhaps spent some of her time at Jack O'Leary's Bar across the street.

The heavy, semitropical air emphasized the warmth of the night. I dropped off to fitful sleep.

At 5:30 I wakened enough to stagger over to the bed. I felt I had never been so sleepy in my life. The persons who had been doing the celebrating had gone home. The street was enjoying an interval of quiet. I sank instantly into deep slumber and almost immediately the bell of the alarm clock pulled me back to wakefulness.

Six-thirty!

I was to meet Bertha Cool at 7:20.

CHAPTER TWO

I FELT CERTAIN the man with Bertha Cool would be the New York lawyer. He was a tall, rangy man in the late fifties with long arms. A dentist had evidently tried to lengthen his face when he made the dental plates.

Bertha Cool was still down to her conservative 165. She'd put on a coat of sunburn from her deep-sea fishing, and the tanned skin contrasted with her gray hair. She came striding toward me with a push of muscular legs that made the New York lawyer lengthen his stride to keep up with her.

4

I moved forward to shake hands.

Bertha gave me a quick glance from those hard gray eyes of hers, said, "My God, Donald, you look as though you'd been drunk for a week."

"It was the alarm clock."

She snorted. "You didn't have to get up any earlier than I did. This is Emory Hale, Emory Garland Hale, our client."

I said, "How are you, Mr. Hale?"

He looked down at me, and there was a quizzical expression on his face as he shook hands. Bertha interpreted the expression. She'd seen it before on other clients.

"Don't make any mistake about Donald. He weighs a hundred and forty with his clothes on, and his jackknife and keys in his pocket, but he's got an oversize brain, and enough guts for an army."

Hale grinned then, and it was just the sort of grin I'd expected. He carefully placed the edges of his teeth together and pulled his lips back—probably just a mannerism, but you kept thinking he was afraid his dental plates would fall out if he gave them a chance.

Bertha said, "Where do we talk?"

"At the hotel. I've got rooms. The town's still pretty crowded—tourist season still on."

"Suits me," Bertha said. "You found out anything yet, Donald?"

I said, "I gathered from the air-mail letter you sent to me in Florida that Mr. Hale was to give me the details so I could start work."

"He is," Bertha said. "I told you generally what he wanted in that letter. You must have been here three days already."

"One day and two nights."

Hale smiled.

Bertha didn't. She said, "You look it."

A taxi took us to a modern hotel in the business part of the city. It might have been any one of half a dozen

5

large cities. There was nothing to indicate the romantic French Quarter which was within half a dozen blocks.

"Did Miss Fenn stay here?" Hale asked.

I said, "No. She stayed at the Monteleone."

"How long?"

"About a week."

"And then?"

"She walked out and never came back, just disappeared into thin air."

"Didn't take her baggage?" Hale asked.

"No."

"Just a week," he said. "I can't believe it."

Bertha said, "I've got a date with a bathtub. You haven't had breakfast, have you, lover?"

I said, "No."

"You look like the wrath of God."

"Sorry."

"You aren't sick, are you?"

"No."

Hale said, "I'll retire to my room and get some of the dust and grime removed. And I think I can do a little better job of shaving than I did at this early hour on the train. I'll see you in—how soon?"

"Half an hour," Bertha said.

Hale nodded and went down the corridor to his own room.

Bertha turned to me. "Are you holding out?"

"Yes."

"Why?"

"I want to find out more things from Hale before I tell him everything."

"Why?"

"I don't know—just a hunch."

"What are you holding out?"

I said, "Roberta Fenn stayed at the Monteleone Hotel. She ordered a package sent C.O.D., a dress she'd had fitted and on which she'd paid a twenty-dollar deposit.

6

There was another ten dollars due. The dress came after she left. It stayed there for about a week, and then the hotel sent it back to the store. They had a record of it on the hotel books."

"Well," Bertha said impatiently, "*that* doesn't tell us anything."

I said, "Three or four days after the dress was returned, Miss Fenn rang up the store, said if they'd send the package down to Edna Cutler on St. Peter Street, Miss Fenn would leave the money with Miss Cutler to pay the C.O.D."

"Who was Edna Cutler?" Bertha asked.

"Roberta Fenn."

"You're certain?"

"Yes."

"How did you find out?"

"The woman who rented the apartment to her identified the photograph."

"Why on earth would Roberta Fenn have done anything like that?" Bertha asked.

I said, "I don't know either. Here's something else." I opened my wallet, took out a personal I had clipped from a morning paper, and handed it to Bertha.

"What is it?" she asked.

"A personal that's been running every day for two years. The newspaper won't give out any information about it."

"Read it to me," Bertha said. "My glasses are in my purse."

I read her the ad: "*Rob F. Please communicate with me. I haven't ceased loving you for one minute since you left. Come back, darling. P.N.*"

"Been running for two years!" Bertha exclaimed.

"Yes."

"You think Rob F. is Roberta Fenn?"

"It could be."

"Shall we tell Hale all this?"

7

"Not now. Let him tell us all he knows first."

"And you aren't even going to tell him about this ad in the agony column?"

"Not yet. Have you got a check out of him?"

Bertha's eyes grew indignant. "What the hell do you take me for? Of course I've got a check out of him."

I said, "All right, let's find out what *he* knows first, and tell him what *we* know a little later on."

"How about that apartment? Can we get in and look around?"

"Yes."

"You're sure?"

"Yes."

"Without arousing suspicion?"

"Yes. I slept there last night."

"*You* did!"

"Yes."

"How did you arrange that?"

"I rented it for a week."

Bertha's face darkened. "My God, you must think the agency's made of money! The minute I turn my back on you, you go around squandering dough. We could have got in there just the same by telling the landlady we wanted to rent it, and—"

"I know," I interrupted, "but I wanted to go over the place with a fine-tooth comb and see if there was anything that she might have left there, any clue to what had happened."

"Did you find anything?"

"No."

Bertha snorted. "You'd have done a lot better to have stayed here and got a night's sleep. All right, get the hell out and let Bertha get cleaned up. Where do we eat?"

"I'll show you a place. Ever had a pecan waffle?"

"A what?"

"A waffle with pecans in it."

"Good God, no! I'll eat my nuts as nuts, and my

waffles as waffles. And I'm going to check out of this hotel and go live in that apartment. We won't have it a dead expense if I do that. When it comes to money matters, you—"

I slipped out into the corridor. The closing door bit off the rest of her sentence.

CHAPTER THREE

HALE PUSHED AWAY HIS PLATE so as to clear a place on the table in front of him. "I'm taking the ten-thirty plane to New York," he said, "so I'll have to talk while Mrs. Cool finishes her waffle—if you don't mind, Mrs. Cool?"

Bertha said, her words thickened somewhat by a mouthful of her second pecan waffle, "Go right ahead."

Hale picked up his briefcase, propped it on his lap, and folded back the flap so he could have ready access to the interior of it.

"Roberta Fenn was twenty-three years old in 1939. That would make her approximately twenty-six at the present time. I have here some additional photographs —I believe Mrs. Cool sent you some photographs by air mail, Lam."

"Yes, I have them."

"Well, here are some additional ones showing her in different poses."

He shot his hand down in the briefcase, pulled out an envelope, and handed it to me. "There's also a more detailed description in there. Height, five feet four; weight, one hundred and ten; hair, dark; eyes, hazel; figure, perfect; teeth, regular; complexion, clear olive, skin very smooth."

Bertha Cool caught the eye of the Negro waitress and beckoned her over. She said, "I want another one of those pecan waffles."

I asked Bertha, "Are you trying to fit those clothes you threw away a year ago?"

She became instantly belligerent. "Shut up! I guess I—" She realized a cash customer was present and bottled up her temper. "I eat only one good meal a day," she explained to Hale with something that wasn't a smile, not yet a smirk. "Usually it's dinner, but if I eat a heavy breakfast and go light on dinner, the result is the same."

Hale studied her. "You're just the right weight to be healthy," he said. "You're muscular and vigorous. It's really surprising the amount of energy you have."

Bertha said, "Well, go ahead with the facts. I'm sorry *we* interrupted you." She glared at me and added, "And I didn't throw those clothes away. I've got them stored in a cedar closet."

Hale said, "Well, let's see. Oh, yes, Roberta Fenn was twenty-three when she disappeared. She was an agency model in New York. She posed for some of the ads, the petty stuff. She never got the best-advertised products. Her legs were marvelous. She did a lot of stocking work —some bathing-suit and underwear stuff. It seems incredible a young woman who had been photographed so much could disappear."

Bertha said, "People don't look at the faces of the underwear models."

Hale went on: "Apparently it was a voluntary disappearance, although we can't find out why. None of her friends can throw any light on it. She had no enemies, no financial troubles, and as far as can be ascertained, there was no reason why she should have vanished so suddenly—certainly not the usual reasons."

"Love affair?" I asked.

"Apparently not. The outstanding characteristic of this young woman was her complete independence. She liked to live her own life. She was secretive about her private life, but her friends insist that was only because she was too independent to have confidants. She was a *very* self-sufficient young woman. When she went out with a man, she always went Dutch, so she wouldn't feel under any obligations."

"That is carrying independence altogether *too* far," Bertha announced.

"Why do you want her now?" I asked. "In other words, why let the case lie dormant for three years, and then get in a dither about finding her, rush detectives down to New Orleans, go flying around the country, and—"

The two rows of regular teeth glistened at me. He was nodding his head and smiling. "A very astute young man," he said to Bertha. "Very smart indeed! You notice? He puts his finger right on the keynote of the whole business."

Bertha's waitress handed her the plate with the waffle. Bertha put on two squares of butter. The waitress said, "There's melted butter in that pitcher, ma'am."

Bertha tilted the pitcher of melted butter over the waffle, piled on syrup, said, "Bring me another pot of *pure* coffee and fill up that cream pitcher." She turned to Hale. "I told you he was a brainy little cuss."

Hale nodded. "I'm very well satisfied with my selection of the agency. I feel quite certain you'll handle the matter satisfactorily."

I said, "I don't want to seem insistent, Mr. Hale, but—"

He laughed aloud. For the moment, his teeth almost parted. "I know. I know," he said. "You're going to come back to the original question. Well, Mr. Lam, I'll tell you. We want to find her in order to close up an estate. I regret that I can't tell you anything else. After all, you know, I am working for a client. I am governed by his wishes. It would be well for you to adopt a similar attitude."

11

Bertha washed down a mouthful of waffle with a gulp of hot coffee, said, "You mean he's not supposed to start backtracking in order to find out what it's all about?"

Hale said, "My client will see that you are given the *necessary* information, and inasmuch as he is in reality your employer—well, I think you can appreciate what an embarrassing circumstance it would be if friction should develop."

Bertha Cool frowned across at me. "You get that, Donald," she said. "Don't go playing around with a lot of theories. You stick to the job in hand. Find that Fenn girl and quit worrying about who wants her. You understand? Forget that romantic angle."

Hale glanced over at me, to see how I was taking it. Then he looked back at Bertha. "That's being put a great deal more bluntly than I'd have said it, Mrs. Cool."

Bertha said, "I know. You'd have done a lot of palavering around. This gets it over with. There's no misunderstanding this way. I don't mince words. I hate beating around the bush."

He smiled. "You're a very direct woman, Mrs. Cool."

There was a moment of silence.

"What else can you tell me about Roberta Fenn?" I asked.

Hale said, "I gave Mrs. Cool most of the details while I was on the train."

"How about close relatives?" I asked.

"She had none."

I said, "Yet you're trying to find her to close up an estate?"

Hale put a big hand on my arm in a fatherly gesture. "Now, Lam," he said, "I thought I'd made myself clear on that."

"You have," Bertha said. "Do you want daily reports?"

"I should like them, yes."

"Where will you be?"

"In my New York office."

"Suppose we find her, then what?"

Hale said, "Frankly, I doubt if you will. It's a cold trail, and a tough assignment. If you do find her—I shall be *very* much pleased. You will, of course, let me know at once. I feel certain my client will make some substantial acknowledgment by way of a bonus."

Hale looked around cautiously. "I feel that I should tell you: Don't do any talking. Make your inquiries casual. If you have to ask direct questions, ask them in such a way as not to arouse suspicion. Pose as a friend of a friend. You happened to be coming to New Orleans, and your friend suggested you should look up Roberta Fenn. Make it casual and entirely natural. Don't be too eager, and don't leave any back trail."

Bertha said, "Leave it to us."

Hale looked at his watch, then beckoned the waitress. "The check, please."

CHAPTER FOUR

BERTHA COOL looked around the apartment, peering here and there into odd corners as a woman will.

"Darn good antique furniture," she said.

I didn't say anything, and after a moment she added, "If you like it." She walked over to the windows, looked out on the balcony, turned back to look at the furniture, and said, "I don't."

"Why not?" I asked.

She said, "My God, Donald, use your head! For years I was weighing around two hundred and seventy-five pounds. Somebody was always inviting me out to dinner and throwing a Louis the Quinze chair at me, some damn spindle-legged imitation of a narrow-seated, lozenge-backed abortion in mahogany."

"Did you sit in them?" I asked.

"Sit in them, hell! I wouldn't have minded so much if the hostesses had used their heads, but none of them did. They'd lead the crowd into the dining-room, and then *I'd* stand and look at what had been assigned as a parking place for my fanny. In place of doing anything, the nitwit hostess would stand there, looking first at me and then at the damn chair. You'd think it was the first time she'd realized I had to sit down when I ate. One of them told me afterward she just didn't know what to do, because she was afraid I'd feel conspicuous if she had the maid bring me another chair.

"I told her that wouldn't make me feel half as conspicuous as sitting down on one of those gingersnaps on ornamental stilts and having the damn thing fold up with me like a collapsed accordion. I hate the stuff."

We prowled around the apartment some more. Bertha Cool picked a studio couch, tried it tentatively, then finally settled back, opened her purse, fished out a cigarette, and said, "I don't see we're a damn bit nearer what we want than when we started."

I didn't say anything.

She scraped a match on the sole of her shoe, lit the cigarette, glowered at me belligerently, and said, "Well?"

I said, "She lived here."

"What if she did?"

"She lived here under the name of Edna Cutler."

"What difference does that make?"

I said, "We know where she lived. We know the alias she was using. During the time she was here, there was a lot of rain in New Orleans. She'd be eating out. Particularly on the rainy days, she wouldn't go very far. There are two or three restaurants within two blocks of the place. We'll cover those and see what we can find out."

Bertha glanced at her wrist watch. I got up, walked over to the door, and went out.

There was a flight of noisy stairs down to a patio, then a long passageway. I made a right-angled turn past another patio, and came out on Royal Street. I walked down to the corner and saw a sign, *Bourbon House.* I walked over there.

It was typical of the real French Quarter restaurant—not the tourist-trap affairs that put on a lot of glitter and charge all the traffic will bear, but a place where the prices were low and the food good. There were no frills or la-de-dah, and the place catered to regular customers.

I knew I'd struck pay dirt. Anyone who was living in that section of the Quarter would hang out there pretty regularly.

I walked over to the door that led to a bar, then turned back to the room that had the lunch counter, a couple of pinball machines, and a juke box.

"Want something?" the man behind the counter asked.

"Cup of pure coffee and some nickels for the pinball machine," I said, tossing four bits on the counter.

He handed me the nickels and drew off the coffee.

Two or three men were hanging around one of the pinball machines, giving it a good play. I gathered from their conversation they were regulars around the place. The juke box clicked into noise. A feminine voice said, "May I have your attention, please. This song is dedicated to the management." Then the juke box started playing *Way Down Upon the Swanee River.*

I took from my pocket the pictures Hale had given me. Just as I tasted the coffee, I gave an exclamation of disgust.

"What's the matter?" the man behind the counter asked. "Something wrong with the coffee?"

"No," I said. "Something wrong with the photographs."

15

He looked puzzled, but sympathetic.

I said, "The photographer gave me the wrong ones. I wonder where *mine* are."

There was no one else at the counter at the moment. The man leaned across the bar, and I casually swung the pictures around so he could take a look.

I said, "I suppose now I'm out of luck. They'll have mixed the films up, given mine to someone else, and I'll never see them again."

"Perhaps they just switched the orders," he said. "You got this girl's pictures, and she got yours."

"That isn't going to help any. How am I going to find her?"

He said, "Say, I've seen that girl! I think she used to eat in here once in a while. Wait a minute. I'll ask one of the boys."

He motioned to the colored waiter, handed him one of the pictures. "Who's this girl?" he asked.

The waiter took the picture, turned it toward the light, and said instantly, "Ah don' know her name, but she ate heah about two-three years ago quite regular. Ah don' think she comes heah no mo'."

"Left town?" I asked.

"No, suh. Ah don' rightly think so. Ah seen her on the street about a month ago. She just ain't been in heah, that's all."

I said, "Well, there's a chance the photographer may know. She seems to have been in there recently with this roll of pictures. They're nearly all of her."

"Ah'll tell you where Ah seen her," the colored boy said. "Ah seen her about a month ago comin' out of Jack O'Leary's Bar. Somebody was with her."

"Man?" I asked.

"Yes, suh."

"You didn't know the man?"

"No, suh, Ah don'. He was a tall man with kinda big hands, carryin' a briefcase."

"How old?"

"Maybe fifty, maybe fifty-five. Ah don' remember rightly, suh. He was a stranger to me. Ah just happened to remember the girl and that she didn't eat here no mo'. Ah used to wait on her when she was here."

"Can you tell me anything more about this man?" I asked.

The waiter thought for a minute, then said, "Yes, suh."

"What?"

"He looked like he was holdin' somethin' in his mouth," he said.

I didn't press the inquiry any further. I paid for the coffee, went over and stood watching the boys who were playing the pinball machine, and after a few minutes walked out.

I went down to Jack O'Leary's Bar. At this hour there wasn't so much of a crowd. I climbed up on one of the stools and ordered a gin and Seven-Up.

The bartender brought my drink, waited on another customer, then drifted over my way.

"What's the picture?" I asked, showing him the photograph.

"Huh?"

I said, "It was here on this stool next to me, face down. I thought it was a piece of paper and was going to crumple it up. Then I saw it was a photograph."

He took a good look at it and frowned.

I said, "She must have dropped it here—must have been someone who was here a minute ago, sitting on that stool."

He shook his head, even while he was trying to think, said, "No. She wasn't there a minute ago, but I've seen her. Wonder how that picture got there. She was in here —seems like it was quite a while ago. I'm certain she hasn't been in today."

"Know her?" I asked.

He said, "I know her when I see her, but I don't know her name."

I put the picture in my pocket. He hesitated a moment as though debating the ethics of the situation, then moved away.

I finished my drink and went out to stand on the street corner, thinking things over.

I put myself in the position of a young woman—hairdresser, manicure, cleaning and dyeing.

There was a beauty shop across the street and part way down the block. A woman who seemed bubbling over with good-natured friendliness came to the door when she saw me fumbling around with the knob.

"What is it?" she asked.

I said, "I'm trying to find out something about a woman. She's a customer of yours," and pushed the best picture of Roberta Fenn in front of her.

She recognized the picture instantly, said, "She hasn't been here for as much as a couple of years, I guess. She used to come in quite regularly. I can't think of her name now, but she was a good customer—came down here from Boston or Detroit or some place up north. I think she was looking for work when she first came here, and then she didn't seem to worry about it any more."

"Perhaps she got a job."

"No. She didn't. She used to come down weekdays around the middle of the day. I used to see her going out for breakfast around eleven o'clock, sometimes not until afternoon."

"You don't know whether she's still in town?"

"I don't think she is, because she'd have been in. We were friends—well, you know, she liked my work and liked to talk with me. I think she was—say, why do you want to know?"

I said, "I—well—she's a nice girl. It means a lot to me —I should never have lost track of her."

"Oh." She smiled. "Well, I wish I could help you, but I can't. I've got a customer in there. In case she shows up again, do you want to leave a message for her?"

I shook my head and said, "If she's in town, I'll find

her myself," and then added with a little smile, "I think it would be better that way."

"It would for a fact," the woman said.

I trudged on down the street to a cleaning establishment. It was a combination residence and business place, with a counter half across the front room. I pulled out the picture, said, "Know this girl?"

The woman who was in charge of the place looked at the picture, said, "Yes. She used to place a lot of work through me. That's Miss Cutler, isn't it?"

"Yes. Know where she is now?"

"No, I don't—that is, I can't tell you where she's living."

"She's here in town, isn't she?"

"Oh, yes. I saw her on the street about—oh, let me see, I guess it was about six weeks ago. I don't get uptown very often. This place keeps me tied down. I can't leave it unless I have someone else to put in charge."

"What street?" I asked.

"Canal. It was—let me see, it was just about five-thirty in the evening, and she was walking down the street. I don't think she recognized me. I have a pretty good memory for faces, and I see lots of my customers when I'm out on the street." She smiled. "Lots of times they know they've seen me before, but can't place me, because they've been accustomed to seeing me behind the counter here. I never speak to them unless they speak to me."

I thanked her and went back to the apartment. Bertha Cool was lounging back in a chair, smoking a cigarette, with a glass of Scotch and soda on the little table by the side of the chair.

"How you doing?" she asked.

"Not too good."

"Like hunting for a needle in a haystack," Bertha said. "My God, Donald, I've found the most wonderful restaurant."

"Where?"

"Right up the street here."

"I thought you'd had your one meal for. the day. I didn't know you were hungry. I just came back now to see if you wanted something to eat."

"No, lover, not now. I find I get along better if I don't let myself get *too* hungry. Just eat a little something to take the keen edge off my appetite."

I nodded and waited.

A dreamy look of satisfaction came over Bertha's face. She all but smacked her lips. "Gumbo with rice," she said, "I thought it would be light."

"Was it?"

"It was a meal, but *what* a meal."

"Had enough?" I asked. "Want to go out for a bite to eat with me now?"

"Don't you say food to me again, Donald Lam! I've had my quota for the day. I'll have some tea and toast tonight and that'll be all."

I said, "Well, I'm going to grab a bite to eat and stay on the job."

"What can I do?"

"Nothing yet."

Bertha said, "I don't know why I'm here."

"Neither do I."

She said, "That lawyer insisted on my coming. He said that after you'd found her I could talk with her better than you could. He had the money to pay for it, and since he was giving the party, I decided to attend."

"That's right."

Bertha said, "It would be swell if we could get that bonus."

"Wouldn't it!"

"How do things look?"

"I can't tell yet. Well, I'm on my way."

I went back to Royal Street and walked down toward Canal, picking my way along the sidewalk which had been paved years ago by embedding huge, flat-surfaced rocks in the dirt and connecting them with cement.

Some of the rocks had sunk more than others. Some of them had tilted slightly. The general effect was artistic, but not conducive to blind walking.

I was halfway to Canal Street when the idea struck me. I went into a telephone booth and started calling the business colleges.

The second one gave me everything I needed. No, they didn't know any Edna Cutler, but a Miss Fenn had taken a course and had been a very apt pupil. Yes, they'd been able to place her. She was in one of the banks. She was secretary to the manager. Just a minute and they'd give me the address.

It was that simple.

The manager of the bank was a human sort of chap. I told him that I was trying to get some information which would enable me to close up an estate and asked him if I might talk with his secretary. He said he'd send her out in a few minutes.

Roberta Fenn looked exactly like her pictures. She was perhaps twenty-six from the standpoint of statistics, but she looked around twenty-two or perhaps twenty-three. She had a quick smile, clear, alert eyes, and a well-modulated, pleasant voice. "Something that you wanted to know?" she asked. "Mr. Black said you were trying to close up an estate."

"That's right," I said. "I'm an investigator. I'm trying to find out something about a man who's connected with a family named Hale."

Her eyes showed me I'd drawn a blank.

I said, "He has a relative whose name I don't know, but I believe you're acquainted with him. I'm not certain exactly how he's related to Hale."

"You don't know this man's name?"

I said, "No."

She said, "I don't have a very wide circle of acquaintances here."

I said, "This man is tall. He has a high forehead, rather bushy eyebrows, and his hands are very thin with

21

long, tapering fingers. His arms are long. He's about fifty-five."

She was frowning thoughtfully as though searching her mental card index.

I watched her closely, said, "I don't know whether it's just a habit or whether his teeth don't fit. Whenever he smiles, he—"

I saw the expression change on her face.

"Oh," she said and laughed.

"You know who I mean?"

"Yes. How did you happen to come to me?"

I said, "I heard he was in New Orleans and someone said he was going to look you up on a matter of business."

"But you don't know his name?"

"No."

She said, "Archibald Smith is his name. He's from Chicago. He's in the insurance business up there."

"Do you have his Chicago address?"

"Not with me," she said. "I have it written down at home."

"Oh!" I let my face show disappointment.

"I could look it up and have it for you tomorrow."

"That would be fine. Have you known him long, Miss Fenn?"

She said, "No. He came to New Orleans about three or four weeks ago and was here for a couple of days. A friend of mine had given him a letter to me—asked me to show him around a little bit, and I showed him some of the more typical sights—you know, the restaurants and bars and things a tourist wants to see."

"The French Quarter?" I asked.

"Oh, yes."

I said, "I suppose that's rather an old story to you people who live here, but it's interesting to the tourists."

She said, "Yes," noncommittally.

I said, "I'd like very much to get in touch with Mr.

Smith. I feel quite certain that he's related to the party I'm looking for. I wonder if it would be possible for me to get that information this evening."

"Why—I could get it for you after I went home."

"Do you have a telephone?"

"No. There's a booth in the building, but it's hard to call *in* there. I could call *out* all right."

I glanced at my wrist watch, a glance which brought her back to the realization that she was a working girl and this time was being taken from the bank. I saw her shift her position uneasily as though anxious to get the interview over with.

I said, "I don't want to be persistent. Is your apartment near here?"

"No. It's pretty well out on St. Charles Avenue."

I said suddenly, "Let me be here with a taxicab when you get off work. You can jump in the taxi, and I'll drive down to your apartment house. You can give me the information I want. It won't take you as long to go down in a cab as it does in a streetcar, and—"

"All right," she said, "I'm off work at five."

"The bank will be closed then?"

"Oh, yes."

"Where shall I meet you—if the bank isn't open?"

"Right by that street door over there."

I said, "Thank you very much, Miss Fenn, and I appreciate what you've done very much."

I raised my hat, walked out of the bank, went up to the hotel, put a *Do Not Disturb* sign on my room, rang up the telephone operator, told her to call me at 4:30, and tumbled into bed for a two-hour sleep.

CHAPTER FIVE

ROBERTA FENN was on time to the minute. She came out looking trim, tailored, and cool. Her steady, hazel eyes were amused about something, as though there were a joke she might have shared if she'd wanted to.

I motioned to the cab driver who was waiting at the curb, and he jumped out and held the door open for us.

Settled back against the cushions, Roberta flashed me a quick glance and said, "So you're a detective?"

"Uh huh."

She said, "I'd always had ideas about detectives."

"What sort of ideas?"

"Oh, big, powerful men who try to browbeat you, or sinister people in disguises."

"It's hardly safe to generalize."

"You must have an exciting life."

"I guess I do, if you stop to think of it that way."

"Don't you sometimes?"

"What?"

"Stop to think of it that way."

"Probably not in the way you point out."

"Why?"

I said, "I don't think you ever really stop to analyze the sort of life you're leading unless you're dissatisfied with it. I like my work. Therefore, I take everything for granted, and don't contrast my sort of life with other kinds."

She thought for a long time then, and said, "I guess you're right."

"What?"

"About never thinking about your life unless you're

dissatisfied with it. How long have you been a detective?"

"Seems like a long while," I said.

"Did you start out to be one?"

"No. I started out to be a lawyer."

"What stopped you? Couldn't you complete your education?"

"No. I got admitted to the bar."

"Then what?"

I said, "Some people unadmitted me."

"What do you mean?"

"I found a hole in the law by which a man could commit a murder and thumb his nose at the authorities."

"What happened?" she asked, all breathless interest.

I said, "They disbarred me."

"I know, but what happened after you worked out the way of committing the murder—you know what I mean."

"I'm not certain that I do."

"Did someone commit it and get away with it?"

"It's a long story."

"I'd like to hear it sometime."

I said, "When they disbarred me, they told me I was crazy, that my scheme wouldn't hold water, that it was just a pipe dream, but that it showed a dangerous, antisocial type of mind."

"Then what?"

"Then," I said, "I went out and proved it to them."

"Who committed the murder?"

"They thought I did."

She looked at me abruptly. "Say, are you taking me for a ride?"

"Only in a taxicab."

Those steady, hazel eyes of hers kept looking right through me. She said, "Darned if I don't believe you."

"You might as well. I have nothing to gain by lying."

"Then what did they say—the people who had told you it was a crazy scheme?"

"Oh, they got committees from the bar association together and started amending the laws to try and plug up the loophole."

"Did they do it?"

"In a way—as well as they could by state laws. This loophole is in the Constitution. You can't plug that simply by state laws."

"Can't you tell whether it's plugged or not?"

"No."

"Why not?"

"Because you can't tell what the Supreme Court's going to do."

"Don't they follow regular rules?"

I said, "They used to be bound by precedents. On those matters, we knew what the law was. Now they're changing those old decisions. That throws the whole list out, because you can't tell which ones they'll change and which ones they'll let stand."

"Isn't that dangerous?"

"It may be good, or it may be bad. It's a condition. We've had a shake-up in the law. Eventually these new judges will get the law changed around to suit *their* ideas. Then lawyers will know pretty generally how to advise clients. In the meantime there's a lot of guessing. . . . What can you tell me about Mr. Smith?"

She laughed and said, "You *do* change the subject with disconcerting suddenness, don't you?"

"Was it disconcerting?" I asked.

"Wasn't it intended to be?"

"No."

"What do you want to know about him?"

"Everything you know."

"That's very little. I'll tell you when we get to my apartment."

We drove for several blocks in silence.

"You look terribly young," she said.

"I'm not."

"About twenty-five?"

"Older than that."

"Not much older."

I didn't answer that one.

"You work for someone?"

"I did for a while. Now I have a half interest in the business. Could we talk about something else for a change? New Orleans? Politics? Your love life, perhaps?"

She looked at me searchingly and with no trace of a smile. "What about my love life?"

I said, "I gave you a choice of several subjects to talk about. You didn't get touchy about any one except your love life. Are you trying to cover up something? And that is what's known as a counteroffensive."

She thought that over for a minute. I could see the smile coming back to twitch the corners of her lips. "I guess you're pretty smart, all right. That was *very* well done."

I took a package of cigarettes from my pocket. "Want one?"

She looked at the brand. "Please."

I jiggled a cigarette halfway out. She took it, tapped it on her thumb, and waited for my light. We lit our cigarettes off the same match. The cab slowed down. She looked out of the window, said, "It's the next place, over here on the right."

"Want me to wait?" the cab driver asked as I paid him off.

I looked at Miss Fenn. "Do I?"

She hesitated for just a fraction of a second, then said, "No," and added hastily, "You can always pick up another one."

"I can wait ten minutes without putting it on the meter," the cab driver explained. "It's fifty cents up here, and it'll be fifty cents back. If your—"

"No," Roberta Fenn said firmly.

He touched his cap. I gave him a two-bit tip and followed her across the sidewalk, up a short flight of stairs, watched her open the mailbox, pull out two letters, glance at the return addresses hastily, drop the letters into her purse, and then she was fitting a key to a door.

It was a walk-up. Her apartment was on the second floor. There were two rooms, both small. She indicated a chair, said, "Sit down. I'll try to find that letter from my friend, asking me to show Mr. Smith around. It may take me a little while."

She went on through into the bedroom and closed the door.

I settled down in the chair, picked up a magazine, held it open so I could bury myself in it at an instant's notice, and made a mental survey of the apartment.

She hadn't been there long. The place hadn't as yet taken on any of her individuality. There were a few magazines on the table. Her name printed on the back of one showed she was a subscriber. Yet there were no back copies visible in the apartment. I'd have bet money she hadn't been living there more than six weeks.

It was about five minutes later that she emerged triumphantly from the bedroom. "It took me a little while," she said, "but I have it—only it doesn't give the room number. I thought it did. It gives the name of the building."

I took out my notebook and fountain pen.

She unfolded the letter. From where I sat, it looked like a woman's handwriting. She said, "Archibald C. Smith is in—oh, shucks!"

"What's the matter?"

She said, "His office building isn't given here. I thought it was. I'll have to look it up in my address book. I thought it was in the letter. I remember now, he gave me his address just before he left, and I wrote it down in my address book. Just a minute."

She took the letter with her, re-entered the bedroom, and popped out a second or two later turning the pages of a small, leather-covered address book. She dropped the letter on the table.

"Yes. Here it is. Archibald Collington Smith, Lakeview Building, Michigan Boulevard, Chicago."

"Room number in there?"

"No. That's where I was confused. I knew I didn't have the number, just the building."

"You said he was in business there?"

"Yes. That's an office building. I haven't his home address."

"What did you say his business was?"

"Insurance."

"Oh, yes. I wonder if your friend might be able to tell me something about him." I motioned toward the letter.

She laughed, and I knew she'd been baiting a trap. "I presume she could, but if you're really looking for Mr. Smith to close an estate, I imagine Mr. Smith can tell you all you need to know about Mr. Smith."

I said, "Doubtless he could," and then added, "That's one of the troubles we sometimes encounter, particularly when we're dealing with a name as common as Smith. You know, a man will try to make it appear he's the person you're after, hoping he can get the money. That's why we always like to investigate as many different angles as possible before we approach him directly."

Her eyes were smiling at me, and then suddenly she was laughing. "That was a splendid recovery, but you must take me for an awful simp."

"What now?"

She said, "It's the first time I ever heard of anyone trying to find a missing heir by that sort of an approach. Usually, some lawyer says, 'Now before we can close up the estate, we have to find an Archibald C. Smith who was the son of Frank Whoosis who died in nineteen hundred and umpty. The last we heard of Smith was that he was in Chicago, running a haberdashery store.' So then the detectives start looking, and one of them comes to me, and says, 'Pardon me, Miss, but do you happen to know a Mr. Smith who is in Chicago running a haberdashery store?' And I say, 'No, but I know a Mr. Smith who's in Chicago in the insurance business. What does the man you want look like?' And the detective says, 'Good Heavens, I don't know. All I'm looking for is a name.' "

"So what?" I asked her.

"That's what I'm asking you."

"You mean that this is unusual?"

"Yes. Very."

I smiled and said, "Isn't it?"

There was exasperation on her face. She was getting ready to let me have a verbal broadside when knuckles sounded on the door. She let her attention swing from me to the door, regarding it with a puzzled frown.

The knuckles sounded again.

She got up and walked over to the door, flung it open.

A man's voice, sharp-edged with eagerness, said, "I told you you couldn't run out on me! But you had to try it, didn't you? Well, sweetheart, I—"

I wasn't looking toward the door right then, but when his voice ran out of words, I knew he'd been pushing his way into the room as he talked, and had advanced just far enough to get a glimpse of me sitting there in the chair.

I turned my head casually.

I recognized him almost instantly. It was the man who had responded to all the horn-blowing at Jack O'Leary's Bar around three-thirty that morning.

Roberta Fenn whirled, glanced at me, then said in a low voice to her visitor, "Come outside for a minute where we can talk."

She half pushed him out into the hallway, and pulled the door behind her so that it was almost shut.

I had only a few seconds. I knew I must make every move count.

I raised myself gently from my chair so as not to make any noise. My hand snaked out and grabbed the letter which Roberta had left on the top of the table.

The envelope bore the return address: *Edna Cutler, 935 Turpitz Building, Little Rock, Ark.*

I gave the letter a quick once-over. It read:

Dear Roberta: A few days after you receive this, you'll have a call from Archibald C. Smith of Chicago. I've given him your name. For business reasons, I wish you'd be particularly nice to him and make his stay in New Orleans as pleasant as possible. Show him around the Quarter and take him to some of the famous restaurants. I can assure you it will be bread on the waters, because—

I heard the door opening from the corridor, heard a man's voice saying, "All right then, that's a promise. Don't forget, now."

I tossed the letter back to the table and was putting a match to my cigarette when Roberta Fenn came back.

She smiled at me, said, "Well, let's see. Where *were* we?"

"Nowhere in particular," I said. "Just talking."

She said, "You're a detective. Tell me how that man could have got through the street-entrance door without ringing my apartment."

"That's easy."

"How?"

"He could have rung one of the other apartments, got a signal to come in, and then gone up. Or he could have picked the lock on the lower door. The locks on those street doors don't amount to much. They're made so that the key to any apartment will open them. Why would he *want* to get in without giving you a ring?"

She laughed, a nervous, high-pitched little laugh, and said, "Don't ask me why men *want* to do the things they do. Well, I guess I've told you everything I know about Archibald Smith."

I took the hint, got to my feet, and said, "Thanks a lot."

"You're—you're here in town?"

"Yes."

"Oh."

31

I headed off any further questions by saying abruptly, "I suppose I've interfered with your evening. I hope I haven't made you late—"

"Don't mention it. You haven't interfered at all. Thank you."

She stood at the doorway and watched me down the flight of stairs. I went out through the outer door, looked up and down the street, sized up the cars that were parked near by, but couldn't see the tall chap who had busted in on Roberta Fenn.

I had plenty of opportunity to look around, too. It was ten minutes before I was able to pick up a cab which was running empty back toward town. The cab driver assured me I was lucky. Cabs, he said, didn't do much cruising around in that part of town.

CHAPTER SIX

MY FEET ON THE STEEP, WOODEN STAIRS sounded like a herd of horses walking over a wooden bridge. I fitted my latchkey and opened the door of the apartment.

Bertha Cool was stretched out in the easy chair. Her thick, capable legs were thrust out straight in front of her, the feet propped on a cushioned ottoman.

She was snoring gently.

I switched on the lights in the center of the room. Bertha slept on peacefully, her face relaxed into a smile of cherubic contentment.

I said, "When do we eat?"

She awoke with a start. For a moment she was blinking the lights out of her eyes, taking in the strange surroundings, trying to find out where she was and how she'd got there. Suddenly realization dawned, and her hard little eyes glittered into mine. "Where the hell have *you* been?"

"Working."

"Well, it's a wonder you wouldn't let me know."

"I'm letting you know now."

She snorted.

"What have *you* been doing?" I asked gently.

Bertha said, "I never was so damn mad in my life."

"What happened?"

"I went to a restaurant."

"Again?"

"Well, I thought I'd better look around. I don't know how long I'm going to be here, and I've heard so much about some of the famous places in New Orleans."

"What happened?"

"The food was wonderful," Bertha said, "but the service—" She snapped her fingers.

"What was wrong with it? Wasn't there enough of it?"

"There was too damn much! It was one of those places where the waiters try to make you feel on the defensive. They treat you as though you were a worm in an apple. 'Now, Madame should have this,' " she said, in an attempt to imitate a waiter speaking with a French accent. " 'Madame will, of course, want white wine with the fish, and red wine with the meat. Perhaps, if Madame is not familiar with the vintages, Madame will accept my selection?' "

"What did you tell him?" I asked, grinning.

"I told him to go to hell."

"Did he?"

"He did not. He hovered around the table, sputtering and telling me what I should eat. I wanted some tomato catsup on my steak, and what do you think he told me? He told me that he wasn't allowed to bring tomato catsup for steaks. I asked him why not, and he said because it would hurt the chef's feelings. The chef made such a marvelous sauce; it was world-famous. Putting catsup on steaks was only done by the very crude persons who had no palate."

"And then?"

"Then," Bertha said, "I pushed back my chair and told him if the chef was so damned solicitous about the steak, he could eat it. And to present the check to his chef along with the steak."

"And you walked out?"

"Well," Bertha said, "they stopped me before I got to the door. There was quite a fuss. I finally compromised by paying for the part of the dinner I'd eaten. But I was damned if I'd pay for the steak. I told them that belonged to the chef."

"Then what?"

"That was all. I started back here, but stopped in at a little restaurant up on the corner, and *really* enjoyed myself."

"The Bourbon House?"

"That's it. Damn these places where they try to put the customer on the defensive."

"They want you to realize you're eating in a world-famous place. They cater only to the élite," I pointed out.

"The hell they do! The place was jammed with tourists. They're the ones the place caters to. Phooey! Telling me what I'm going to eat and what I'm not going to eat, and then expecting me to pay the bill. Famous eating place, eh? Well, if you ask me—"

I settled down on the studio couch, reached for a cigarette, said, "Can you reach Hale by telephone in New York?"

"Yes."

"At night?"

"Yes. I've got his residence number, as well as his office number. Why?"

I said, "Let's go back to the hotel and call him."

"What do you want to call him about?"

"To tell him we've found Roberta Fenn."

Bertha jerked her feet down off the cushion. "I don't suppose this is one of your attempts at being funny?"

"It isn't."

"Where is she?"

"In an apartment house down on St. Charles Avenue, the Gulfpride."

"Under what name?"

"Her own."

Bertha said softly, "Fry me for an oyster! How did you do it, lover?"

"Just leg work."

"There's no question it's this same girl?"

"She matches her photographs."

Bertha heaved herself up out of the chair. "Donald," she said, "you're wonderful! You certainly *do* have brains! You're marvelous! How did you do it?"

"Just running down a lot of clues."

She said, with genuine fondness in her voice, "I don't know *what* I'd do without you. You're marvelous, lover! I mean you *really* are! You—why, dammit to hell!"

"What's the matter?"

Her eyes glittered. "This damned apartment. You said you rented it by the week?"

"Yes."

"We can't get any money back if we move out."

"I guess not."

"Well, of all the damn fools! I might have known you'd do something like that. Honestly, Donald, I sometimes think you're crazy when it comes to money matters. We'll probably be leaving here tomorrow, and here we are stuck with this apartment for a whole week."

"It's only fifteen bucks."

"Only fifteen bucks," Bertha said, her voice rising. "You speak as if fifteen dollars were—"

I said in a low voice, "Hold it. People coming up the stairs."

She said, "I think that's the outfit on the second floor. There's a man and woman who—"

The steps paused abruptly. Knuckles sounded on our door.

I said hurriedly, "Answer the door. It's your apartment from now on."

Bertha marched across the apartment, her heels pounding the floor. She put her hand on the doorknob, paused, and asked, "Who's there?"

A man's voice, cultured, well modulated, said, "We're strangers. We'd like to ask you a question."

"What about?"

"I think it would be better if you opened the door so we didn't have to shout."

I could see Bertha thinking things over. There were two of them, whoever they were. Long training had made Bertha cautious. She sized me up as though wondering just how much help I'd be in a fight, then slowly opened the door.

The man who made a smiling bow was evidently the owner of the well-modulated voice. His companion, standing a pace or two behind, wouldn't go with that type of voice.

The man in front held his hat in his hand. The man behind kept his hat on, his eyes studying Bertha Cool, taking in every detail of her appearance. Abruptly he saw me, and his eyes jumped to mine with a startled quickness which indicated apprehension.

The man who had been doing the talking said, "You'll pardon me, I'm certain. I'm trying to get some information, and I think perhaps you might be able to help me."

"More probably not," Bertha said.

He wore a suit of clothes which had netted some tailor at least a hundred and fifty berries. The hat he was holding in his hand was a pearl-gray Homburg which had set him back around twenty bucks. Everything about the man spoke of quiet class. He seemed to have dressed with the scrupulous care he'd have taken in arraying himself for an Easter-morning parade. He was slender, graceful, suave.

The man who was standing behind him wore a suit which was in need of pressing. It was a ready-made, obviously tailored for a man of different build, and re-tailored in a haberdashery fitting room. He was in the fifties, barrel-chested, tall, tough, and watchful.

The man with the well-modulated voice was saying quite persuasively to Bertha, "If we could step inside for just a moment, we'd prefer that the other tenants in the building didn't hear what we're discussing."

Bertha, blocking the door, said, *"You're* doing the talking. I don't give a damn how many people hear me listen."

He laughed at that, a cultured laugh which showed genuine amusement. His eyes took in Bertha's gray-haired belligerency in a survey which showed awakening interest.

"Go ahead," Bertha said, irritated at his appraisal. "Either drop a nickel or hang up."

He took a card case from his pocket with something of a flourish, jerked a card halfway out as though intending to give it to Bertha Cool, then let it stay there. "I'm from Los Angeles. My name is Cutler, Marco Cutler."

I looked at Bertha's face to see if she got it. From all I could see, she hadn't.

Cutler said, "I am trying to get information concerning my wife."

"What about her?" Bertha asked.

"She lived here."

"When?"

"As nearly as I can tell, it must have been around three years ago."

Bertha, caught off guard, said, "Oh, you mean she— that is—"

"Exactly. Right here *in this apartment*," Cutler said.

41

37

I moved foward. "Perhaps *I* can be of some assistance. I'm subletting the apartment to this lady. She's just moving in. Do I understand that you were living here also?"

"No. I was in Los Angeles, carrying on my work. My wife came on here and had this address. As I understand it, she lived in this very apartment."

He whipped some folded papers from his inside pocket, unfolded them, looked at something, nodded, and said, "That's right."

The big man standing behind him seemed to feel called upon to say something.

"Dat's right," he agreed.

Cutler turned to him quickly. "This *is* the place, Goldring?"

"This is the place. I was standing right here when she opened—"

Cutler interrupted hastily: "I appreciate, of course, that it's a forlorn chance, but I couldn't locate the landlady tonight, and I was thinking that perhaps you might have been here for some time, might have known something of the previous tenants, and would be willing to help me."

Bertha said, "I've been here about five hours—"

I laughed and said, *"I'm* the one that's been here for some time. Wouldn't you gentlemen care to come in and sit down for a moment?"

"Thank you," Cutler said. "I was hoping you'd suggest that."

Bertha Cool hesitated a moment, then stood to one side of the door. The two men came in, glanced quickly at the bedroom, walked across to the room which looked out on the balcony over the street.

Goldring said, "That's Jack O'Leary's Bar over there."

Cutler laughed. "I recognized it, but I was trying to reconstruct in my mind the roundabout method by which we arrived. The street seems to be running about ninety degrees off."

Goldring said, "You'll get used to it," appropriated the comfortable chair in which Bertha had been sitting, raised his feet to the ottoman, and said, "Don't mind if we smoke, do you, lady?"

He scratched a match on the sole of his shoe before Bertha had a chance to reply. She said, rather shortly, "No."

Cutler said, "Won't you be seated, Miss—or is it Mrs.?"

I interrupted hurriedly before Bertha could give her name, "It's Mrs. Won't you *gentlemen* be seated?"

Goldring shifted his eyes and looked at me through cigarette smoke as though I'd been a fly crawling along the top of a piece of pie he had intended to eat.

Cutler said, "I'm going to be frank with you—very frank. My wife left me some three years ago. Our domestic life hadn't been entirely happy. She came here to New Orleans. It was only after some difficulty that I found her."

"Dat's right," Goldring said. "I sure had to woik on dat dame."

Cutler went on, in that velvet-smooth voice, "The reason that I was so anxious to find her is that I'd come to the conclusion our marriage would never again be a happy one. Much as I regretted to do so, I decided to divorce her. When love ceases to exist, marriage becomes—"

Bertha sat down uncomfortably on the studio couch, interrupted to say, "Forget it! You don't need to palaver around with me. She left you, and you decided to change the lock on the door so she couldn't come back. I don't blame you. What's that got to do with me?"

He smiled. "You'll pardon me if I comment upon your refreshing individuality. Yes, I won't bother about mincing words, Mrs.—er—"

I said, "Okay then, let's get to the point, because *we* were just going out to dinner. You decided to file suit for divorce. I take it Goldring here found her and after he found her, served the papers."

"Dat's right," Goldring said, looking at me with puzzled respect as though trying to find out how I knew.

"And now," Cutler said with a subtle note of indignation creeping into his voice, "years after the matter has been entirely disposed of, I understand my wife is intending to claim the papers were not actually served upon her."

"Indeed," I said.

"Exactly. It is, of course, preposterous. Fortunately, Mr. Goldring remembers the occasion very vividly."

"Dat's right," Goldring said. "It was about three in the afternoon on the thoiteenth of March, 1940. She came to the door, an' I asked her was her name Cutler an' did she live here. She said she did. I'd found out before de apartment was rented to Edna Cutler. Then I asked her was her name *Edna* Cutler, an' she said, 'Yes,' an' then I took the original summons, the copy of the summons, an' a copy of the complaint, an' I soived the papers on her right while she was standing in that door."

Goldring motioned toward the door which led to the hall.

Cutler said, "My wife now claims that she wasn't even in New Orleans at the time. However, Mr. Goldring has identified a picture of her."

Bertha started to say something, but I nudged her leg with my knee, cleared my throat, frowned at the carpet as though trying to recall something, and said, "I take it, Mr. Cutler, what you want to do is to prove definitely that it *was* your wife who was living in this apartment?"

"Yes."

"And was soived with papers," Goldring said.

I said, "I have been here only a short time, on *this*

trip; but I'm quite well acquainted around New Orleans, and I've been here several times. I think I was here two years ago. Yes, I think it was exactly two years ago. I was living in an apartment across the street. Perhaps *I* could identify Mrs. Cutler's picture."

His face lit up. "That's exactly what we want. People who can prove that she was living here at the time."

He flashed a slender, smooth-skinned hand to the inside of his coat, emerged with a small envelope. From this he took three photographs.

I studied the photographs a long time. I wanted to be certain I'd know this woman when I saw her again.

"Well?" Cutler asked.

I said, "I'm just trying to place her. I've seen her somewhere, but I *don't* think I have ever met her. I've seen her before. That's certain. I can't remember whether she had this apartment. It may come to me later."

I nudged Bertha to get a good look at the pictures. I needn't have bothered. Cutler reached out his hand for the photographs. Bertha snatched them from me and said, "Let's take a good look at her."

We studied the pictures, looking at them together. I have a habit of trying to reconstruct character from photographs. This girl was about the same build as Roberta. The faces were only vaguely similar. Roberta had a straight nose, eyes that could be quizzical or thoughtful. This girl looked more of the light-headed, light-hearted type. She would laugh or smile or cry just as the mood happened to strike her, but she wouldn't have thought about what was coming next. Roberta might laugh, but she'd be thinking while she was laughing. Roberta wouldn't let herself go—not all the way. She'd always have a hand on the emergency brake somewhere. This girl in the picture was a reckless gambler. She'd risk everything on the turn of a card, would take it for granted if she won, and would have stared in stupefied disbelief if she'd lost. She'd never consider the possibility of losing while she was gambling. Roberta

41

was the type who would never risk anything on a gamble that she couldn't afford to lose.

So far as build and figure and complexion were concerned, it looked as if they were sufficiently similar to wear each other's clothes.

Bertha handed the pictures back to Cutler.

"Seems rather young," I said.

Cutler nodded. "She's ten years younger than I am. I suppose that may have had something to do with it. However, I don't want to bore you with my troubles. I came here to see if I could get some proof that she was living here. I should be able to find someone who knows."

"I'm sorry I can't be of more help," I told him. "Perhaps it will come to me later on. Where can I reach you?"

He gave me his card, *Marco Cutler, Stocks and Bonds, Hollywood.* I put it in my pocket and promised I'd communicate with him if I found myself able to remember anything more about the tenant that had been in the apartment three years ago.

Goldring said, "I'm in the telephone book. Give me a ring if you get any dope before Mr. Cutler goes back. An' if you've got any papers you want soived, give me a chance at 'em."

I said I would, then to Cutler, "Can't you force your wife to admit she was here? It would seem that she'd have to show all the details of where she was—if she claims the papers weren't served."

Cutler said, "That is not as easy as it sounds. My wife is inclined to be rather baffling and secretive. Well, thank you very much."

He nodded to Goldring. They got up. Goldring gave a quick look around the apartment and started for the door. Cutler paused. "I don't know how to thank you for your co-operation," he said. "I realize, of course, that something which seems very grave and very important to me is a minor matter to a person who knows none of the parties. I certainly appreciate your courtesy."

When the door had closed behind them, Bertha turned to me. "I *like* him," she said.

I said, "Yes. He does have a pleasing voice, and—"

"Don't be a damn fool," Bertha said. "Not Cutler. Goldring."

"Oh."

"Cutler is a damn mealy-mouthed hypocrite," Bertha announced. "No one who's that polite can be sincere about it, and being insincere is just another way of being a damn hypocrite. Goldring is the one I like. He doesn't beat around the bush with a lot of palaver."

I tried imitating Goldring's voice. "Dat's right," I said.

Bertha glared at me. "At times you can be the most exasperating little shrimp that ever wore out good shoe leather. Come on. Let's call Hale. He should have reached New York by this time. At any rate, we can leave a call for him."

CHAPTER SEVEN

WE SAT IN THE HOTEL waiting for the telephone call to be completed. Central had reported that no one was at Hale's office, and the house as yet hadn't answered.

Bertha said into the telephone, "We don't know just what time he'll get home. It'll be sometime tonight. Keep trying."

I said to Bertha, "*I* want something to eat while we're waiting. It's my dinner time."

Bertha wouldn't think of letting me go out. "I want you here when this call comes through. Have something sent up."

43

I told her it would probably be midnight before we heard from him, but had a waiter bring up a menu. Bertha looked it over, and decided she'd have a shrimp cocktail while I was having my steak dinner.

"You know I just *can't* sit and watch you eat," she said.

I nodded.

The waiter seemed solicitous. "Just a shrimp cocktail?" he asked.

"What are those oysters Rockefeller?" Bertha inquired.

"Baked oysters," he said, his face lighting with enthusiasm. "The shells are placed in hot rock salt. There's a little touch of garlic and a special sauce. That sauce is something of a secret. And then they're baked, right in their shells."

"It sounds good," Bertha said. "I'll try half a dozen—no, make it a dozen. Put some French bread in the oven, toast it brown, put on lots of melted butter, and bring me a pot of coffee with a big pitcher of cream and lots of sugar."

"Yes, madam."

Bertha glowered at me. *"Pure* coffee," she snapped.

"Yes, madam. Some dessert?"

"Well, I'll see how I feel when I get done with that," Bertha said.

After the waiter had gone, Bertha looked at me, waiting for me to say something. When I didn't, she brought it up herself. "After all," she said, "you can only put on just so much weight in any one day. I see no reason for counting calories, now that I've already put all the food into my system it can possibly absorb for one day."

I said, "It's your life. Why not live it the way you want?"

"I think I will."

There was silence for a few moments; then she said in a low voice, "Look, lover, there's something I want to say to you."

"What?"

She said, "You're a brainy little cuss, but you don't know a damn thing about money. It takes Bertha to handle the finances."

"What now?"

Bertha said, as though afraid she was starting an argument, "Since you left Los Angeles, we've gone into a new business."

"What is it?"

There was that cunning look on Bertha's face which comes when she's putting something over. "The B. Cool Construction Company. I'm the president and you're general manager."

"What do we construct?"

"Right now," Bertha said, "we're working on a military housing job. It's a very small job, something that we can handle all right. You won't need to bother with it much. It's a subcontract."

"I don't get it," I said.

Bertha said, "I thought we shouldn't have too many eggs in one basket. You can't tell what's going to happen, the way things are going now."

"But why pick up this construction job?"

"Oh, I just saw an opportunity to get in on something."

"That doesn't sound convincing to me." I waited.

Bertha took a deep breath. "Dammit," she said, "I've got a lot of executive ability. Since you came in as a partner, I have been doing too much deep-sea fishing. Sitting out there on the barge, and thinking about the way that young boys are dying, just because us older folks haven't carried out our share of the responsibility— Well, we've gone into this construction business, and that's all there is to it. Don't bother too much about it. I'll call on you from time to time for anything I need, but for the most part Bertha can handle it."

The telephone rang before I could say anything.

Bertha snatched up the receiver with an eagerness

which showed how much she welcomed the interruption. She held it to her ear, said, "Hello. . . . Oh, hello—I was trying to get you. Where are you . . . No, no. *I* was trying to get *you* . . . Oh, you did. Well, isn't that strange? Well, tell me what you have to say first. . . . Oh, all right, if you insist. Better brace yourself. We've got some news for you. . . . That's right. We've found her. Down at the Gulfpride Apartments on St. Charles Avenue. . . . No. The Gulfpride. G-u-l-f-p-r-i-d-e. That's it. . . . Oh, that's a professional secret. We've got our way of uncovering leads. It was a pretty cold trail, but we've been working like dogs ever since you left. You'd be surprised at the number of leads we've run down. . . . No, I haven't talked with her yet. Donald did. . . . Yes, my partner, Donald Lam."

There was an interval during which I could hear the rasping, metallic sound of his voice coming through the telephone transmitter. Bertha sat there and listened. She said, "Well—yes—I guess I can."

She looked at me, hurriedly thrust her palm over the transmitter, and said, "He wants me to go down there and see her early in the morning."

"Why not?"

She hastily removed her hand from the mouthpiece, said, "Yes, Mr. Hale, I understand," clapped her palm back over it, and said, "He wants me to cultivate her, win her confidence, pump her."

"Watch out," I warned. "She's no one's fool. Don't guarantee any particular results."

Bertha said into the transmitter, "Well, that will be fine, Mr. Hale. I'll be very glad to do the best I can. . . . Yes, I'll take Donald with me. We'll leave early in the morning, just as soon as she's up. She doesn't go to work until nine, and that means she'd leave the house about eight-thirty. We could be waiting to pick her up with a cab. What is it you want me to tell her?"

There was another interval during which the metallic sounds of the telephoned instructions were almost audible. Then Bertha said, "Very well, Mr. Hale, and I'll let you know. Do you want me to wire you or . . . I see. All right. Well, thank you. Thank you very much. *We* think we're pretty good, too. . . . Yes, I told you he was short on weight, but long on brains. Well, good night, Mr. Hale—oh, wait a minute. When they ring you on my call, tell them the call is canceled. They have a great way of trying to put through two calls by trying to get you to talk on my call as well as on yours. I'll ring up and cancel it, but don't let them stick you by making you think it's another call. . . . All right, good-by."

Bertha hung up the telephone, jiggled the receiver, said, "Hello, hello. Hello, Operator. This is Mrs. Cool in Mr. Lam's room. . . . Yes, that's right, Mr. Lam's room. . . . No, I checked out and have my baggage in Mr. Lam's room. That's right. I had a call in for Mr. Hale at New York. Cancel it. That's right. Cancel it. . . . No, I just talked with him. . . . Well, it was on *his call*. . . . Oh, hell, cancel it and don't go prying into—just cancel it!"

Bertha slammed up the receiver, turned to me, and said, "My God, the telephone company must ride these girls every time a call gets canceled. You'd think I was jerking the food out of their mouths. His plane was grounded somewhere. I didn't get the name of the place. Where the hell do you suppose our food is? I—"

The waiter tapped discreetly on the door.

"Come in," I said.

Bertha doesn't like to talk when she's eating. I let her go ahead and eat.

"What time do you want to try Roberta Fenn?" I asked when she pushed her plate back.

Bertha said, "I'll get up and come to the hotel. I'll be here at seven o'clock. You be in the lobby all ready to go. Now be *certain* you're there. I don't want to do any waiting around, with a taxicab meter clicking. The minute you see me drive up, hop out, and *get in the car*. Seven o'clock. Understand?"

"On the dot," I told her.

Bertha sat back with a smile of calm contentment, and blew smoke up at the ceiling.

The waiter appeared with a menu. Bertha didn't even bother to look at it. "Bring me a double chocolate sundae," she ordered.

CHAPTER EIGHT

BERTHA SEEMED SURPRISED when she saw me coming out to meet her cab as it pulled in at the curb, promptly at seven o'clock. Her diamond-hard eyes were glittering angrily at the world.

"Did you sleep well?"

"Sleep!" she said and made it sound like an expletive.

I gave the cab driver the address out on St. Charles Avenue. "What's the matter?" I asked. "Was it noisy?"

She said, "When I was a girl, women used to let their seductions be carried on usually with secrecy, and always in silence."

"Why? What's the matter? Did you hear a seduction last night?"

"Did I hear a seduction!" Bertha exclaimed. "I heard a whole damn medley of seductions. I realize now why they talk about the young man of today tomcatting around. When they say that they don't mean a guy's prowling around so much as that he's getting out in some public place and yowling about it."

"I gather that you didn't sleep well."

Bertha said, "I didn't. I can assure you of one thing, though."

"What?"

"I gave a group of young women a lungful of advice from that balcony."

"How did they react?"

Bertha said, "One of them got mad. One of them looked ashamed and went home, and the others stood there and laughed at me—starting to pass wisecracks right back at me."

"What did you do then?" I asked.

"I blasted 'em," Bertha said with a vicious snap of her words.

"Did they stay blasted?"

"No."

I said, "No wonder you didn't sleep."

Bertha said, "It wasn't the noise. I was just too damned mad to sleep. The idea of little hussies prowling around the street with no sense of shame. Oh, well, we live and learn."

"Are you going to check out of that apartment?" I asked.

"Check out of it!" Bertha exclaimed. "Don't be a fool! *The rent's paid!*"

"I know, but after all there's no use staying in an apartment where you can't sleep."

Bertha's lips came together in a firm, straight line. "Sometimes I could grab you and shake the teeth out of you. One of these days your damned extravagance will bust this partnership."

"Are we going broke?" I asked.

"We won't go into all that again," Bertha said hastily. "You've been lucky. Some day you'll quit being lucky, then you'll come whining to me, asking me to put up cash to finance the partnership over a tough spot. Right then's when you'll learn something about Bertha Louise Cool, and don't you ever forget it."

I said, "It's an intriguing thought. It makes the possibility of bankruptcy sound almost alluring."

She deliberately averted her head, pretending to stare

out at the scenery along St. Charles Avenue. After a moment she said, "Got a match?"

I handed her a match and she lit a cigarette. We rode in silence until we came to the Gulfpride Apartments.

"Better have the cab wait," I told Bertha. "It's hard to get a cab here. We may not be long."

"We're going to be quite a while," Bertha said, "a lot longer than you think. We aren't going to have any taxi meter playing tunes while we're talking."

Bertha opened her purse, paid off the cab driver, and said, "Wait here until after we've rung the bell. If we get a buzz to go on up, don't wait. Otherwise, we'll go back with you."

The cab driver looked at the ten-cent tip Bertha had given him, said, "Yes, ma'am," and sat there, waiting.

Bertha found the button opposite the name of Roberta Fenn and jabbed her thumb against it with sufficient force to make it seem she was trying to flatten the bell button.

"Probably isn't up yet," Bertha snorted. "Particularly if she was out last night. I wouldn't doubt if she was one of them that was making that whoopee under my window. Apparently things don't really get going in this town until around three o'clock in the morning."

She speared the button with another vicious thumb jab.

Abruptly the buzzer on the door made noise. I pushed against the door, and the door moved inward. Bertha turned and waved dismissal at the taxicab driver.

We started up the stairs, Bertha pushing her chunky hundred and sixty-five pounds with slow deliberation up the steep flight, I moving along behind her, letting her set the pace.

Bertha said, "When we get up there, lover, you leave the talking to me."

"Know what you're going to talk about?" I asked.

"Yes. I know what he wants me to find out. Think

they have the steepest stairs in the world in New Orleans—damned outrage!"

I said, "It's the second one on the left."

Bertha wheezed up the last few stairs, marched down the corridor, raised her knuckles to tap on the door, and stopped, holding her hand motionless for a half second as she noticed that the door was open about a half inch. She said, "Evidently she wants us to walk right in," and pushed the door open.

"Wait a minute," I said, and grabbed her arm.

The door swung open under the impetus of the push Bertha had given it. I saw a man's feet propped at a peculiar angle. The swinging door gradually brought the body into view, a body that was sprawled half on and half off a chair, the head down on the floor, one foot hooked up under the arm, the other leg bent around the arm support. A sinister red stream had flowed from a hole in his left breast down across the unbuttoned vest, down through the cloth of the coat, to spread out in a pool on the floor. A singed soft cushion showed how the shot had been muffled.

Bertha said under her breath, "Fry me for an oyster!" and took a quick step forward.

I still had hold of her arm. I used all my strength to pull her back.

"What's the idea?" Bertha said.

I didn't say anything, just kept pulling.

For a moment she was angry; then she caught a glimpse of the expression on my face and I saw her eyes widen.

I said, in a rather loud tone of voice, "Well, I guess there's no one home, after all." All the time I was tugging at her arm, dragging her toward the stairs.

Once she got the idea, she moved quickly enough. We moved silently along the carpeted corridor, and I all but pushed Bertha past the head of the stairs, where she wanted to stop and argue.

We pell-melled out onto the street, and I pulled Bertha back against the wall and started walking rapidly down St. Charles Avenue.

Bertha collected her thoughts sufficiently to start pulling back. "Say, what's the idea?" she asked. "What in the world's got into you? That man was murdered. We should have notified the police."

"Notify the police if you want to," I said, "but don't be dumb enough to think you could have gone into that room and come out alive."

She stopped walking to stand stock-still, her feet rooted with surprise, staring at me. "What on earth *are* you talking about?" she demanded.

"Don't you get it?" I asked. "Someone pressed the buzzer for us to come on up. Then that someone left the door slightly ajar."

"Who?" she asked.

I said, "You have two guesses. Either the police were in there waiting for someone to show up, which, under the circumstances, is rather unlikely, or the murderer was waiting patiently to claim his second victim."

Her hard little eyes stared at me, fairly sparkling with the intensity of her thought. She said, "Pickle me for a peach! I believe you're right, you little bastard."

"I know I'm right."

"But it's hardly possible that *we* could have been the ones he was laying for."

"We would have been," I said, "once we entered that room."

"What do you mean?"

"We'd have seen who he was then. We might not have been the ones he expected, but once we got in there, he couldn't afford to let us get out—not after we'd seen his face."

I saw Bertha's color change as she realized the narrow escape she'd had. She said, "And that was why you were doing all that talking about no one being in?"

"Certainly. There's a restaurant across the street. We'll telephone the police from there and also keep a watch on the apartment so we can see anyone who comes out."

"Who was that person?" Bertha asked. "Do you know him—the dead man?"

"I've seen him before."

"Where?"

"He came to call on Roberta Fenn last night. I think his visit was unexpected and unwelcome—and I'd seen him once before that."

"Where?"

"The other night. I couldn't sleep. I walked out on the balcony. He was just coming out of a bar across the street. Two women were with him, and someone was waiting for them in an automobile."

Sudden recollection of the night before stabbed at Bertha's memory. She said, "Was it one of the horn-blowing brigade?"

"The instigator of the damnedest horn-blowing of the evening," I told her.

She said simply, "I'm glad he's dead."

"Shut up! It's dangerous to joke about such things."

"Who in hell said I was joking? I mean every word of it. Don't we have to notify the police?"

I said, "Yes. But we do it my way."

"How's that?"

I said, "Come on. I'll show you."

We went into the restaurant. I asked very loudly if I could get the proprietor to telephone for a taxicab, or should I telephone for one.

He motioned toward a phone booth, and gave me the number of the cab company. I went back and called the cab office. They assured me a cab would be there within two minutes. From the booth I could watch the door of Roberta Fenn's apartment house.

I waited until I heard the horn of the cab outside the restaurant, then dialed police headquarters, and said very casually, "Got a pencil?"

"Yes."

I said, "The Gulfpride Apartments on St. Charles Avenue."

"What about them?"

"Apartment two-o-four," I said.

"Well, what about it? Who is this talking? What do you want?"

"I want to report that a murder was committed in that apartment. If you'll rush some radio cars down there, you *may* catch the murderer waiting for another victim."

"Say, who is this talking?"

"Adolf."

"Adolf who?"

"Hitler," I said, "and don't ask me anything else because I've got a mouthful of carpet." I hung up the phone, and walked out.

Bertha had walked out to hold the taxicab. I came sauntering after her as though there was no particular hurry.

"Where to?" the cab driver asked.

Bertha started to give him the name of the hotel, but I beat her to it, and said, "Union Depot. No hurry. Take it easy."

We settled back against the cushions. Bertha wanted to talk. I jabbed my elbow into her ribs every time she started to say anything. Finally she gave it up, and sat glowering at me in seething, impotent rage.

We paid off the cab at the depot. I piloted Bertha through one entrance, swung her around, and out another. "Monteleone Hotel," I told the driver.

Once more I held Bertha to silence. I felt as though I were holding down the safety valve on a steam boiler. I didn't know at what moment an explosion might occur.

We arrived at the Monteleone Hotel. I escorted Bertha over to a row of comfortable chairs, settled her in the deep cushions, sat down beside her, and said quite affably, "Go ahead and talk. Talk about anything in the world you want to—except anything that's happened in the last hour."

Bertha glared at me. "Who the hell are you to tell me what to talk about and what not—?"

I said, "Every move we've made up to this point will be traced. It's what we do from here on that really counts."

Bertha snapped, "If they trace us here, they'll trace us the rest of the way."

I waited until the clerk's eye drifted our way; then I got up, walked over to the desk, smiled affably, and said, "I believe the bus comes here to pick up passengers for the plane north, doesn't it?"

"Yes. It will be here in about thirty minutes."

"It's all right for us to wait here for it?" I managed to seem meek and uncertain of myself.

"Quite all right," he assured me, smiling.

I rejoined Bertha. After the clerk's attention was diverted elsewhere, I strolled over to the newsstand. A few moments later I gave Bertha a signal to join me; then we walked around to the entrance to the drugstore. I stopped long enough to play a pinball machine; then we were out on the street.

"Where to?" Bertha asked.

"The hotel first—long enough to get packed up and checked out."

"Then where?"

"Probably the apartment."

"Both of us?"

"Yes. That studio couch can be made into an extra bed."

Bertha said, "What's the idea? You're running away as though *you'd* done it."

"Don't be too certain the police won't think so."

"Why?"

I said, "Roberta Fenn was working in a bank. They'll ask the banker what he knows. He'll say that yesterday afternoon a man came to see her, claiming to be an investigator trying to clean up an estate. Roberta Fenn talked with him. The young man was waiting for her at the bank when she got off work. He put Roberta in a taxicab, and they drove off. The young man was in her apartment when the man who was murdered called last night. The man was jealous."

"Where's Roberta while all this was going on?" Bertha Cool asked.

"Roberta," I said, "is, one, the one who pulled the trigger on the gun, or, two, sprawled out on the floor where we couldn't see her without going into the room, or, three, the person for whom the murderer is waiting."

Bertha said, "I think the thing to do is to get into a taxicab, go down to police headquarters, and tell them the whole circumstances."

I stopped, swung her around to the curb, and pointed to a cab that was parked on the opposite side of the street. "There's a cab," I said. "Get in."

Bertha hesitated.

"Go ahead."

"You don't think so, do you, Donald?"

"No."

"Why not?"

"There are lots of reasons."

"Name some."

I said, "It stinks."

"What does?"

"The whole business."

"Why?"

I said, "Hale came to Los Angeles. He hired us to come to New Orleans and find Roberta Fenn. Why didn't he get a New Orleans detective agency on the job?"

"Because he had confidence in us. *We'd* been recommended to him."

"So rather than get a New Orleans detective agency for a routine job, he pays us a fancy price, *and* traveling expenses, *and* a per diem from Los Angeles here."

"You were already in Florida. He seemed to be pleased when I told him that. I told him you could be here a couple of days before we arrived."

"All right, he was pleased. He hired us to come in and work on this case because he had confidence in us. *And he knew where Roberta Fenn was all the time.*"

Bertha stared at me as though I'd done something utterly incomprehensible like tossing a brick through the plate-glass window in the drugstore behind us.

"It's the truth," I said.

"Donald, you're absolutely crazy! Why should a man come all the way to Los Angeles and hire us at fifty dollars a day with an extra twenty for expenses, to find a woman in New Orleans whom he said was missing, but who wasn't?"

"*That,*" I said, "is the reason *I'm* not getting in any taxicab and going to police headquarters. You may if you want to. There's the cab, and knowing you as I do, I feel quite certain you have enough money to pay the fare."

I started walking toward the hotel.

Bertha came striding along after me. "You don't need to be so damned independent about it!"

"I'm not being independent. I'm simply keeping my nose clean."

"What are you going to say when the police do get hold of you and make things tough because you didn't report the murder?"

"I did report the murder."

She thought that over.

"The police aren't going to like it, just the same."

"No one asked them to."

"When they finally get their hands on you," Bertha warned, "it's going to be *just too bad!*"

"Unless we can give them something else to distract their attention."

"Such as what?" she asked.

"The murderer who was in that room, or, perhaps, a brand new murder case. Something that will keep their minds occupied."

Bertha automatically fell into step with me, thinking things over.

She said at length, "Donald, you're crazy about that Hale business."

"What about it?"

"About him knowing where Roberta Fenn was."

"He had already found her."

"What makes you think so?"

I said, "The waiter at The Bourbon House saw her coming out of Jack O'Leary's Bar with Hale."

"You're certain?"

"Reasonably so. The waiter described him to a T, said he looked like he was holding something in his mouth."

"When was this?"

"About a month ago."

"Then *she* knows who Hale is?"

"No. Hale knows who she is. *She* thinks Hale is Archibald C. Smith of Chicago."

Bertha sighed. "This is too damn much for me. It's one of those Chinese puzzles that *you* like. *I* don't like them."

"I'm not crazy about this one myself. This isn't a question of whether we like it or not. It's something we're in—right up to our necks."

Bertha said, "Well, I'm going to get in touch with Hale and call for a showdown. I'm—"

"You're going to do nothing of the sort," I interrupted. "You'll remember that Hale told us he didn't want us making any investigation as to why we were hired, or who had hired us. We were hired only to do one thing, to find Roberta Fenn."

I could see that Bertha was thinking things over all the way to the hotel. Just before we entered the lobby, she said, "Well, I've made up my mind to one thing."

"What?"

"We've found Roberta Fenn. That's what we were hired to do. And we collect that bonus. Now I've got to get back to Los Angeles. That construction-company business is important."

I said, "It's okay by me."

Bertha entered the lobby, marched up to the desk, and said, "When's the next train out of here for California?"

The clerk smiled and said, "If you'll inquire at the porter's desk, he'll— Wait a minute. Aren't you Mrs. Cool?"

"Yes."

"You were registered here. Checked out last night, didn't you?"

"That's right."

The clerk said, "A telegram came in for you this morning. We sent it back to the telegraph company. Just a moment. Perhaps it hasn't gone out yet. No. Here it is."

He picked it out and handed it across to Bertha Cool.

She tore it open and held the message so I could read over her shoulder. It was dated Richmond the night before and read: *After talking with you on telephone have decided return New Orleans first available plane. Emory G. Hale.*

CHAPTER NINE

WE MOVED AWAY from the desk. Bertha kept staring at the telegram. I said, "He'll be here almost any time now. There's an early plane gets in from New York. He didn't say just what plane he'd take, did he? Richmond must have been where he was grounded on the trip north."

"No—the first available plane. That was because they're so crowded these days."

I said, "When he comes, I'll do the talking."

Bertha reached a sudden decision. "You're damn right you're going to do *all* the talking. Bertha is bundling herself into an airplane and flying to Los Angeles. In case Mr. Hale asks questions, it's because Bertha has some war work which demanded her presence. You aren't going to tell him anything about having gone down there this morning and about what happened, are you?"

"No."

"That is all I wanted to know," she said.

"Want me to go out to the airport with you to see you off?"

"I do not. You're poison. You're the smarty pants that held out on Hale just because you thought Hale was holding out on you. It's your party. You sent out the engraved invitations, and now you can seat the guests as they come in. Bertha is going over and get some nice pecan waffles, and then be on her way."

"I want a key to the apartment," I said, "and—"

"It'll be in the door. I'll pack my bag and leave my key in the door. Good-by."

She strode to the door, and I watched her get into a taxicab. She didn't even look back.

When the cab had pulled away, I went into the dining-room, had a good breakfast, went up to my room, stretched out in a chair with my feet propped on another chair, and read the morning paper while I was waiting for Hale.

He arrived shortly after ten o'clock.

I shook hands and said, "Well, you certainly made a quick round trip."

He pulled his lips back from his teeth in his characteristic smile. "I did for a fact," he admitted. "I didn't realize I was teamed up with two such fast workers. What happened to Mrs. Cool? I inquired for her, and they said she'd checked out."

"Yes. She was called back to Los Angeles on an emergency—war work."

"Oh," he said. "You're doing work for the F.B.I. then?"

"I didn't say that."

"Well, you intimated as much."

I said, "I'm not familiar with *all* the partnership business, but I don't think we are."

He grinned. "If you were, you wouldn't admit it?"

"Probably not."

"That's all I wanted to know. I'm disappointed she isn't here, however."

"She said there was nothing more she could do. Since Roberta had been located, it was simply a question of cleaning up details."

"Well, in a way, that's right. You certainly are fast workers. They told me at the desk that Mrs. Cool had checked out last night about seven o'clock. She didn't *leave* last night, did she?"

"No. This morning."

"But she checked out last night?"

I said, "That's right. She got an apartment down in the French Quarter. She thought it would be more centrally located for our investigations. She was to stay down there, while I stayed up here."

"Oh, I see. Where is this apartment?"

"I can't tell you exactly. It's one of those apartments where you go in one street, wind around through half a dozen turns and twists, and come out on another. Or are you familiar with the French Quarter?"

"No."

I said, "You'll get a kick out of this apartment. It's typical."

"So Mrs. Cool is doing war work. She didn't tell me that."

"You didn't ask her, did you?"

"No."

I said, "She seldom volunteers information about her business to clients."

He flashed me a quick look. I kept my face absolutely straight.

"She hasn't talked with Miss Fenn then?"

I let my face show that I was surprised. "Why, we understood from your telegram that *you* wanted us to hold off that interview until you came, so you could talk with her."

"Well—not exactly. You say she's living in the Gulfpride Apartments on St. Charles?"

"Yes."

"I'd guess we'd better drive down there. Had breakfast?"

"Oh, yes."

"Well, let's go see her."

"Want me there when you talk with her?"

"Yes."

We called a taxi and gave the address of the Gulfpride Apartments. When we were about halfway there, the driver slid the glass window back, turned, and said, "That's the place where they had the murder this morning, ain't it?"

"What place?"

"The Gulfpride Apartments."

"You can search me. Who was killed?"

"I don't know. Some man name of Nostrander."

"Nostrander," I said, as though trying to recall the name. "I don't believe I know anyone of that name. What did he do?"

"He was a lawyer."

"Sure it was murder?" I asked.

"That's the way I understand it. Somebody plunked him right in the middle of the heart with a thirty-eight caliber."

"Did he live there?" I asked.

"No. He was found in some jane's apartment."

"Like that, eh?"

"I don't know. This girl worked in a bank some-where."

"What happened to her?"

"She's missing."

"Don't happen to remember her name, do you?"

"No, I don't—wait a minute. I heard it, too—one of the boys was telling me about it. Let me see. It was a short name, name of—name of Pen—no, that's not right. Wait a minute. Fenn. Fenn, that was the name. Roberta Fenn."

I said, "Police think she pulled the trigger?"

"I don't know what *their* theory is. All I know is what I picked up from a gabfest we were having down at the stand. One of the boys had had a hurry-up call to pick up a photographer for some pictures of the body. Said it was an awful mess. Well, here's the building. Cars certainly parked all around it."

Hale started to say something. I beat him to it. "What do you say," I asked in a loud voice, "if we go and see this other party first, and then come back for our inter-view at the Gulfpride after the excitement has died down? I don't like to try and carry on a business conver-sation with people running in and out, chasing up and down stairs, making noise and—"

"I think that's a *very* wise decision," Hale said.

I said to the cab driver, "Okay, drive us on down to Napoleon and St. Charles and let us off there." I settled back against the cushions and said in a loud voice to Hale, "Our party at the Gulfpride won't be interested in talking business this morning, anyway. He'll be swap-ping gossip with the other tenants. My idea is we'd bet-ter let him go until afternoon."

"Okay, just as you say."

After that, we were silent until the cab driver let us off at Napoleon and St. Charles.

"Want to have me wait?" he asked.

"No. We'll probably be here for an hour or two."

He took the tip I gave him and drove off.

"Well?" Hale asked.

"We wait for a streetcar and ride back to town."

He showed his excitement. "We want to find out all we can about that case. Look here, Lam, you're a detective. Would it be possible for you to get in touch with the police and find out what they know about—"

"Not one chance in ten million," I interrupted firmly.

"Don't the police and the detective agencies work together?"

I said, "The answer to that is best contained in a one-syllable word of unmistakable meaning. It's *no!*"

"But this raises the devil with all of my plans. You're sure this woman was the same Roberta Fenn whose pictures I showed you?"

"Yes."

Hale said, "I wonder where she is."

"The police are probably asking themselves that same question."

"Do you think you could find her again, Lam?"

"It's possible."

His face lit up. "I mean in advance of the police?"

"Perhaps."

"How would you go about doing it?"

"I can't tell just yet."

We waited by the car tracks. He was nervous, kept glancing at his watch.

A streetcar came along. We swung aboard, and I knew Hale had reached a decision on something by the time we took our seats. He kept looking for an opportunity to break it to me, but I didn't give him any conversational opening for anything. I simply sat looking out the window.

We craned our necks as we went by the Gulfpride Apartments. Quite a few cars were still in front of the place. A little group of men was standing on the sidewalk, heads close together, talking.

That gave Hale the opportunity he wanted. He sucked in a deep breath, said, "Lam, I'm going back to New York. I'm going to leave you in charge here."

I said, "You'd better get a room, hole up, and get some sleep. You can't keep commuting back and forth to New York all the time."

"I'm afraid I wouldn't rest much."

I said, "That apartment Bertha Cool just vacated is wide open. You can move in there and go to sleep. It won't be like a hotel. There won't be anyone to disturb you. You can simply lock your door and pass out."

I could see that the idea appealed to him.

"What's more," I said, "you'll find that apartment interesting for another reason. Roberta Fenn lived there for several months. She was then going under the name of Edna Cutler."

That brought him bolt upright. His eyes, red-rimmed, slightly bloodshot from lack of sleep, were wide with startled interest. "Is that how you found her?"

"I got some clues there, yes."

He seemed a bit worried. "It's uncanny how you find things out, Lam. You're a regular owl."

I laughed at that.

"Perhaps you know a lot more about Miss Fenn than you've told me?"

"You wanted me to find her, didn't you?"

"Yes."

"Well, I found her. We try to give results, and don't bother our clients reporting methods, or talking about clues."

He settled back once more in the car seat. "You're a very unusual young man. I don't see how you found out so much in so short a time."

I said, "We get off here and walk the rest of the way. It'll take five minutes."

Hale was very much interested in the furniture, and the old-fashioned, high-ceilinged rooms. He walked out onto the porch, looked around at the plants, looked up and down the street, came back, tried the bedspring with the palm of his hand, and said, "Very, very nice. I think I'll be able to rest here. And so Roberta Fenn lived here—very, very interesting."

I told him he'd better try to get some sleep, left him there, went out, and hunted up a telephone booth where I'd be assured of privacy.

It took me half an hour dealing over the phone with a detective agency in Little Rock to find out that 935 Turpitz Building, the address given in Edna Cutler's letter to Roberta Fenn, had been a mailing address only. It was a big office where a girl rented out desk space to small businessmen, did stenographic work, and forwarded mail.

She would forward mail to Edna Cutler, but the actual address of her client was confidential—very much of a secret.

I told the Little Rock man the agency would send him a check, and then hunted up a commercial typing agency. I asked the girl in charge, "Could you make a stencil for me and run off a thousand letters on a mimeograph machine?"

"Why, certainly."

"Got a stenographer I can dictate a sales letter to?"

The girl smiled at me, picked up her pencil. "The managing department now becomes the clerical unit. You can start whenever you're ready."

I said, "I'm ready. Here we go."

I started dictating:

Dear Madam:

A close personal friend of yours says that you have pretty legs. You want them to look pretty, and we want them to look pretty.

You can't get the sheer hosiery which you could for-

merly buy—not if you try to buy in the United States.

It is quite possible, however, that exclusive arrangements could be made to supply you with sheer silk hosiery for the duration of the war. At the time of Pearl Harbor a Japanese ship put into a Mexican port and we were able to obtain its cargo of silk stockings originally destined for the United States. This hosiery would be shipped to you duty prepaid from Mexico City. All you'll have to do will be to open the package, put on the stockings, and wear them for thirty days. If, at the end of those thirty days, you are entirely satisfied, make a remittance at the same price you were paying for hosiery a year ago. If any of the hose should develop runs or show signs of defective workmanship or of material, you need only to return such defective hose for a complete credit.

Simply place your name and address, the size, style, and color of sheer silk stocking you prefer to wear on the enclosed blank, put it in the enclosed, stamped, addressed envelope, drop it in the mail. You are not obligated in any way.

The girl looked up. "That all?"

"That's all," I said, "except that it will be signed Silkwear Importation Company, and I'll have to work out a color chart and order blank to enclose."

"How many of these do you want?"

"A thousand. After you have the stencil made, I'd like to see one or two samples before we go ahead with the full thousand letters."

She looked up at me, studying me. "All right. Now, what's the racket?"

I just stared at her, saying nothing.

"Look—there was an embargo on silk a long time before Pearl Harbor, and when did stockings ever come from Japan?"

I grinned. "If the people who get these letters are as smart as you are, I'm out of luck. I'm a private detective.

This is a stall. I'm trying to smoke someone out from behind a blind address."

She looked me up and down. I could see the puzzled surprise in her eyes change to respect. She said, "Okay, you almost took me to the cleaners. So you're a detective?"

"Yes, and don't tell me I don't look like one. I'm getting tired of hearing that."

"It's a business asset," she announced. "You should be proud of it. All right, what's the real dope on these? How many of them do you really want?"

"Just two. Don't make too good a job of it. Smear them up a little as though out of a thousand copies these people were getting the last two. You can address the envelopes. The first is Edna Cutler, 935 Turpitz Building, Little Rock, Arkansas, and the other is Bertha Louise Cool, Drexel Building, Los Angeles."

She laughed, swung the typewriter from the side compartment of her desk, and announced, "It's a good gag. Come back in half an hour, and I'll have 'em ready."

She fed the stencil sheet into her typewriter and started playing a tune on the keyboard.

I told her I'd be back, went out, bought an early afternoon paper, and sat down at the lunch counter to read the account of the murder.

As yet, the newspapers didn't have all the details, but they had enough to hit the high spots. Paul G. Nostrander, a popular young attorney, had been found dead in the apartment of Roberta Fenn. Roberta Fenn was missing. Employed in a secretarial position in a downtown bank, she had failed to show up for work. An examination of her apartment convinced police that if she had fled, she had taken no clothes with her, not even her facial creams, toothbrush, or even her purse. The purse was lying unopened on the dresser in the bedroom. Not only did it contain her money, but her keys as well. Police reasoned, therefore, that she was entirely without funds, without means of re-entering her own apartment. They expected either to find her body sometime within the next twenty-four hours, or that she would voluntarily surrender to the police. Police inclined to two theories. One was that the murderer had killed the young attorney, then forced Roberta Fenn to accompany him at the point of a gun. The other was that the murder had taken place during Miss Fenn's absence from her apartment, that she returned to find the body in much the same position as police had found it, and, in a panic, had resorted to flight. There was, of course, the third possibility, which was that Roberta Fenn had been the one who pulled the trigger on the gun.

Apparently police were inclined to give more credence to the first theory.

Police were making a diligent search for a young, well-dressed man wearing a gray checkered suit who had been waiting for Roberta Fenn when she finished her work at the bank the evening before. Witnesses had seen him escort her into a taxicab. Police had a good description: Height, 5 feet 5½ inches; weight, 130 pounds; hair, dark, wavy; eyes, gray and keen; age, 29; suit, gray, double-breasted; shoes, brown and white sport.

Nostrander had been practicing law for about five years. He was 33 years of age, and among lawyers was noted for his ingenuity as well as his mental agility in the trial of a case. He was a bachelor. Both parents were dead, but he had an older brother, 37, who was employed in an executive capacity with one of the bottling companies. So far as was known, the dead lawyer had no enemies, although he had a host of friends who were shocked to learn of his passing.

The crime had been committed with a .38 caliber police special. Only one shot had been fired, and only one shot had been needed. Doctors said death was almost instantaneous. The position of the body and the distance from the hand of the corpse to the gun which was found lying on the floor made it almost impossible to consider the death as other than deliberate murder. Police were also investigating the theory that the death might have been part of some strange suicide pact, that Roberta Fenn had become too nervous or frightened to carry out her part of the bargain, and so had disappeared.

Police fixed the time of the murder as being almost exactly at 2:32 in the morning. Because a pillow had been held over the gun, the report had been muffled. Only one person had actually heard the shot. That person, Marilyn Winton, a hostess at the Jack-O'-Lantern, had been returning home. She had the apartment directly across the hall from that of Miss Fenn. It had been just as she was fitting her latchkey to the street door to the apartment house that she had heard what she took to be a shot. Two friends, who had driven her home, were waiting at the curb to "see that she got in all right." Miss Winton had immediately returned to their car to ask if either of them had heard a shot. Neither had. Police attached some significance to this, as it indicated that the pillow had muffled the explosion sufficiently to make the single shot inaudible above the sound of the idling motor.

The friends had convinced Miss Winton that she had merely heard a door slam. She had gone on upstairs to her apartment, but still only half convinced that it was not a shot she had heard, had looked at her watch to note the exact time. The time was then exactly 2:37. She estimated it had then been not over five minutes since she had heard the shot.

There was nothing in the paper as to how the police had happened to discover the crime. News of that mysterious telephone call of mine had apparently been deliberately suppressed. The newspaper explained that the police who stumbled upon the murder were "merely upon a routine tour of inspection."

I read the news, smoked a cigarette, and went back up to the public typing agency.

Ethel Wells had pulled a proof of the letter for me.

I read it over.

"You think this will do the work?" I asked.

She said, "It rang the bell with me—as you may have noticed."

"I noticed."

She laughed up at me. "You were *all* eyes, as the saying goes."

I said, "I need an address for the Silkwear Importation Company."

"Three dollars a month entitles you to use the office as a mailing address. You can have as many letters sent here as you want."

"Can I trust your discretion?"

"Which, I suppose, is a nice way of asking if I can keep my mouth shut if someone comes around asking questions?"

"Yes."

"If it's a postal inspector, what do I do?"

"Tell him the truth."

"What's that?"

"That you don't know my name or anything about me."

She turned that over in her mind for a few seconds, then said, "That's an idea. What *is* your name?"

"On the books, it'll be *Cash*. You've added three dollars to your month's income, as well as the price of the typing."

CHAPTER TEN

I WENT BACK to the hotel, went up to my room, opened a fresh package of cigarettes, sat by the window, and did a little thinking.

Bertha Cool was somewhere between New Orleans and Los Angeles. Elsie Brand would be running the office. It looked like a good time to get the information I wanted.

I picked up the telephone and placed a station-to-station call. It took about five minutes to get the call through. Then I heard Elsie Brand's voice, crisp and businesslike, saying, "Hello."

"Hello, Elsie. Donald talking."

The hard, keen edge came off her voice. She said informally, "Oh, hello, Donald. Operator said New Orleans was calling, and I thought it was Bertha. What's new?"

"That's what I want you to tell me."

"How come?"

"Bertha tells me she's gone in for war work."

"Didn't you know?"

"No. Not until she told me."

"She's been working with it for about six weeks. I thought you knew."

"I didn't. What's the idea?"

She laughed and said uneasily, "I guess she wants to make money."

"Listen, Elsie, I've been associating with Bertha long enough so I object to paying long-distance telephone rates for the pleasure of listening to you beat around the bush. *What's* the idea?"

"You ask her, Donald."

"I could get pretty damned peeved about this in a minute," I warned.

"Use your head," she said suddenly. "You're supposed to have brains. Why should Bertha want to get into war work? Why would *you* do it if you were in Bertha's position? Figure it out for yourself, and quit pressing me for information. I've got a job to hold, and you're just *one* of the partners."

"Was it so she could make a claim that would exempt me from military service?"

There was silence at the other end of the line.

"Was it?"

"We're having very nice weather out here," Elsie said, "although I suppose I shouldn't tell you that, because it's a military secret."

"It is indeed?"

"Oh, yes. By suppressing all information about the weather, we've taken a long step toward winning the war. One of the things we're short on is newsprint. The Los Angeles Chamber of Commerce used to use up enough paper telling about the climate to cover with dense forest an area of nine thousand, six hundred and eighty-seven acres, assuming that the trees would be on an average of eighteen inches in diameter and would be growing at distances of ten and six-tenths feet, measuring from the center of the trunks. That assumes that the trees would have an average height of—"

"Your three minutes are up," the operator broke in.

"You win," I told Elsie. "Good-by."

"By-by, Donald. Good luck."

I heard the receiver click at the other end of the line, and hung up.

I sat back with my feet propped on a chair, thinking. The telephone rang.

I picked up the receiver, said, "Hello," and heard a man's voice saying cautiously, "Are you Mr. Lam?"

"Yes."

"You're a detective, having offices in Los Angeles—a member of the firm of Cool and Lam?"

"That's right."

"I want to see you."

"Where are you?"

"Downstairs."

"Who is this?"

He said, "You've met me before."

"Your voice is vaguely familiar, but I don't place you—"

"You will when you see me."

I laughed and said cordially, "Come on up."

I dropped the receiver into its cradle on the telephone, grabbed my hat, topcoat, and briefcase, made certain the key to the room was in my pocket, slammed the door shut, locked it, and sprinted down the corridor. I slowed down as I neared the elevator shaft, walked past the elevators, on down to a turn in the corridor, and waited.

I heard an elevator door slide open, waited a few seconds, and peered cautiously around the corner.

There was only one man. He was hurrying down the corridor. There was something vaguely familiar about the way he held his shoulders, and that came as a surprise to me. I'd have bet ten to one that the call had been from the cops, making certain I was in the room before they started to sew the place up. The fact that this man was alone and that I really knew him was an agreeable surprise; but I didn't start down the corridor until I'd placed him, and I didn't do that until he made the turn to the left.

It was Marco Cutler.

Cutler was knocking at my door for the second time when I joined him. "Oh, good afternoon, Mr. Cutler."

He whirled. "I thought you were in your room."

"Me! Why, I just came in!"

He looked at the briefcase, the hat, the topcoat, said,

"I'd have sworn that I recognized your voice. I called your room just now."

"Must have got the wrong number."

"No. I told the operator very distinctly the room I wanted."

I stepped back from the door and lowered my voice. "And someone answered the telephone?"

He nodded, and I could see sudden apprehension upon his face.

I said, "This may not be as simple as it sounds." I took his arm, and moved away from the door. "Let's go get the house detective."

"You mean—you think there's a burglar?"

I said, "It may be the police frisking the room. You didn't give your name, did you?"

This time I could see the twitching of the little muscle at the corner of his left eye. "No—let's get out of here."

"Suits me," I said. "Keep right on going."

We started walking. He said, "I *thought* your voice sounded a little strange."

"How," I asked, "did you locate me?"

"It's rather a peculiar story."

"Let's hear it."

He said, "I looked up the landlady who owns that apartment. I told her that when you folks were finished with it, I'd like to move in. I said I didn't want to put you out, but that I'd pay double the rent she was getting at the present time. I understood you only wanted it for a week and—"

"Go ahead," I said. "Skip the alibis."

"I explained to the landlady that my wife, Edna, had lived in the apartment. She said Edna had been there for several months around three years ago, that she could look it up, and let me have the exact dates. I told her I'd want her as a witness. I took Edna's picture from my pocket, showed it to her, and asked her to

75

identify it. She said that *wasn't* the woman. Then she got suspicious and wanted to know what it was all about. In the course of the conversation it came out that *you* had appeared on the scene a few days earlier and showed her a picture of the woman who actually had rented the apartment, and that she had identified the photographs for you.

"Naturally, that bothered me. You'll understand why. I went up to the apartment at once, trying to get you. You weren't there. I was excited. I kept pounding on the door. A man told me to go away and stay away. I told him I had to see him at once on a matter of life and death, and finally he grumblingly opened the door. I'd expected to find you there or the heavy-set woman. This man was something of a surprise."

"What did you tell him? How much?"

"I told him that my wife had occupied that apartment some three years ago, that I was trying to check up on it to prove that certain papers had been served on her there, that I'd talked with you, and that I simply must talk with you again."

"What did he say?"

"He said he thought I could reach you at the hotel, that you hadn't said anything to him about it, but that if there was anything I wished investigated, you were a very fine private detective. I think he was trying to get you a job. He praised you to the skies.

"The more I thought it over, the more peculiar it sounded. It began to look to me very much as though you were—well—"

"Trying to slip something over?" I asked.

"Yes."

"So what?"

"So I came to see you."

"That's all?"

"Isn't that enough?"

The elevator cage slid to a stop. I said, "Probably not. We'll talk down in the lobby."

76

"Isn't that terribly public?"

"Yes."

"Then why talk there?"

"Because it's public."

"And how about that person in your room?"

I said, "We'll speak to the house detective."

Cutler wasn't keen about that house-detective idea, but he waited while I summoned the house detective, explained to him that a friend of mine had telephoned my room, that a stranger had answered, and that I thought someone might be prowling through the room. I gave him my key, told him to go up, and take a look.

Then I turned to Cutler. "Okay, now we can talk."

Cutler was frightened. "Look here, Lam, suppose it should be the police?"

"The person in my room?" I asked.

"Yes."

"If it's the police, it's all right. City police sometimes get suspicious of private detectives and want to check up on them. It's something we get accustomed to. You have to learn to take it—and like it."

"But if it *is* the police, they'll come down here, pick you up for questioning, find me talking with you, and—"

I interrupted him with a laugh. "That shows how little you know about this game."

"What do you mean?"

"If it's the police," I said, "they'll tell the house detective to go back and say there was no one in the room. He'll come down here, looking smugly complacent, and say that everything is okay."

"And what will the police do?"

"Fade out of the picture temporarily. They don't like to get caught searching a person's room without a warrant."

Cutler seemed apprehensive. "I wish I could believe you."

"You can. I've been through this before. It's a regular

procedure—all in a day's work."

He turned that over in his mind. "I don't want police messing around with this thing. This is a private matter and I'm going to settle it in my own way."

"Very commendable."

"But if the police should start to question me, certain things would come out that I don't want to have made public."

"Such as what?"

"That divorce, for instance."

I said, "Bosh, that divorce was put through in legal form. It's a matter of public record. The whole set of papers will be on file—"

"I know that," he said, and squirmed.

"Go ahead. What's the rest of it?"

"My wife."

"What about her?"

"Don't you understand?"

"No. I thought you said you didn't know where she was."

"Not *that* wife."

"Oh-oh! You've married again, eh?"

"Yes."

"Puts you in something of a predicament, doesn't it?"

"Predicament is no name for it."

I said, "It sounds interesting. Let's hear some more."

"Edna left me and came to New Orleans. I divorced her and got an interlocutory decree. Those things take time. Love doesn't wait. I met my present wife. We went to Mexico and got married. We should have waited for the final decree. It's one hell of a mess."

"Does your present wife know?"

"No. She'd hit the ceiling if she even suspected. If Goldring *did* serve the wrong woman—well, you know something about the case. What is it?"

"Nothing that would help you."

"I could pay you a lot of money to uncover something that would help me."

"Sorry."

He got up. "Keep it in mind. If in your investigations, you stumble onto something that would help me, I'll be very, very generous."

I said, "If Cool and Lam do anything for you, you won't need to be generous. You'll get a whale of a bill."

He laughed at that, got to his feet, said, "Okay, let's leave it that way!"

We shook hands and he left the hotel.

CHAPTER ELEVEN

THE JACK-O'-LANTERN NIGHTCLUB was typical of dozens of other little nightclubs that clustered through the French Quarter. There was a floor show of sorts, half a dozen hostesses, and tables crowded into three rambling rooms which had been merged together by a process of knocking out doors and making full-length openings where windows had been. Out in front a dozen publicity pictures of the various performers in the floor show were exhibited in a large, glass-covered frame.

It was early, and the place hadn't as yet begun to fill up. There were a few stragglers here and there. A sprinkling of soldiers, some sailors, four or five older couples, evidently tourists, determined to "see the sights" and starting early.

I found a table to myself, sat down, and ordered a Coke and rum. When it came, I stared down into the dark depths of the drink with a lugubrious expression of acute loneliness.

Within a few minutes a girl came over. "Hello, sourpuss."

I managed a grin. "Hello, bright-eyes."

"That's better. You look as though you needed cheering up."

"I do."

She came over and stood with her elbows on the back of the chair opposite, waiting for my invitation. She didn't expect me to get up, and seemed surprised when I did.

"How about a drink?" I asked.

She said, "I'd love one." She looked around as I was seating her, hoping some of the others would notice.

A waiter popped up from nowhere.

"Whisky and plain water," she ordered.

"What's yours?" he asked me.

"I've got mine."

He said, "You get two drinks for a dollar when one of the girls sits at the table with you. Or you get one drink for a dollar."

I handed him a dollar and a quarter and said, "Give my drink to the girl. Keep the quarter for change, and don't bother me for a while."

He grinned, took the money, and brought the girl a medium-sized glass filled with a pale amber fluid.

She didn't even bother to pretend, but tossed it down straight as though performing a chore, then pushed the empty glass out in front of her where it bore eloquent testimony to the fact that she was being neglected.

I reached for it before she could snatch the glass away, and smelled it.

She said, somewhat angrily, "Why is it that all you wise guys think you're being so cute when you do that? Of course it's cold tea. What did you expect?"

"Cold tea," I said.

"Well, you're not disappointed. If my stomach can stand it, you shouldn't kick."

"I'm not kicking."

"Most of them do."

"I don't."

80

I reached down in my pocket, pulled out a five-dollar bill, let her see the figure on it, then folded it so it was concealed in my hand, and slid the hand halfway across the table. "Marilyn in here tonight?" I asked.

"Yes. That's Marilyn, the girl standing up by the piano. She's the big-shot hostess, runs things, and spots us girls around at the different tables."

"She sent you over here?"

"Yes."

"What would happen if we started fighting?"

"We wouldn't. It takes two to make a fight. As long as you were buying drinks, I wouldn't fight. When you quit buying drinks, I wouldn't be here to fight with."

"Suppose we didn't get along?"

"Then you wouldn't be buying drinks, would you?"

"No."

She grinned. "Well, then I wouldn't be here."

"Would Marilyn send you back?"

"No. If you stayed here, she'd try you with another girl. Then if you didn't loosen up, she'd let you sit here and mope all by yourself unless the place got crowded. If it did, and they needed the table, they'd get rid of you. Is that what you wanted to know?"

Her hand slid across toward mine.

"Most of it," I said. "What's your name?"

Her hand hesitated. "Rosalind. What else do you want?"

"How could you get Marilyn to come over here and sit at this table?"

Her eyes narrowed slightly. She looked around the room and said, "I think I could arrange it."

"How?"

"Tell her that you like her style, and kept looking at her instead of playing up to me, that I thought she could hustle a few commission checks on the side before the place filled up. She'd fall for that."

"Think you could do that?"

"I'd try."

Her fingers touched mine. The five-dollar bill traded hands.

"Anything else?" she asked.

"How about Marilyn?" I asked. "Is she a good scout?"

"She's all right, but she's been off her feed for the last four or five weeks. She fell awful hard and had a jolt. A girl's a fool to fall for anybody in this racket."

"How's the best way to get along with her? What's the line of approach?"

"With Marilyn?"

"Yes."

The girl grinned. "That's easy. Buy her drinks and slip her a dollar on the side when no one's looking."

"How about her love affair? That fellow didn't make her by buying her drinks, did he?"

"No. A man who buys her drinks is a sucker to her—say, mind if I tell you something?"

"Go ahead."

"I'm going to give you a tip. You look like a right sort. Don't monkey with Marilyn."

"I want something from her."

"Don't get it."

"I mean information."

"Oh."

There was silence for a little while. I caught the waiter looking at me and motioned him over. I handed him another dollar and a quarter and said, "Another drink for the lady."

"You shouldn't have done that," she said after he left.

"Why not?"

"Because Marilyn might not fall for that line I'm going to hand her. That would only go where you're *not* buying me very many drinks. If you kept on buying me drinks, she'd know darn well I wouldn't give a hang who you looked at."

"Mercenary, eh?" I asked, smiling.

She said, "You're damn right I'm mercenary. What did you think this was, love at first sight?"

I laughed.

She said somewhat wistfully, "It may be at that. You're a good kid. You can always tell them, the fellows that treat us like ladies. . . . Marilyn's turning around. Start staring at her. I'll pretend I'm sore."

I stared at Marilyn. She was rather tall, slender, with very dark hair, somewhat deep-set black eyes, and a mouth made up so that the lips were a thick, crimson smear across the olive of her face.

I saw her start to turn away, then suddenly turn back, and realized that the girl at my table had given her some sort of a signal.

For a moment she looked full at me, and I caught the impact of her dark, feverish eyes; then she turned away, standing so that I could see the long curves of her body beneath the red gown which clung to her like wet silk.

Rosalind said, "She's feeling pretty low today. She was a witness on that murder case."

"You mean the lawyer that was killed?"

"Yes."

"The deuce! What did she know about it?"

"She heard the shot—just as she was opening the door of her apartment house."

"And the realization that she had heard the shot that caused the death of someone upset her?" I asked.

"Not Marilyn. She was upset because the officers woke her up to question her, and she lost some of her beauty sleep."

"Does she drink?" I asked.

The girl looked at me suddenly, said, "You're a detective, aren't you?"

I raised my eyebrows in a gesture of surprise. "Me, a detective?"

"Yes, you are. You want to talk with her about that shooting, don't you?"

I said, "I've been accused of lots of things in my life,

but I think this is the first time anyone has taken a good look at me and said I looked like a detective."

"You are, just the same. Okay, you're a good sort. I'll give you a tip. Marilyn Winton is as cold as an electric icebox, but she's accurate. If she says that shot was fired at two-thirty, it was fired at two-thirty, and you don't need to waste time worrying about it."

"But you will get her over here so I can talk with her?"

"Uh huh. And that makes me feel better."

"What does?"

"Your being a detective. I thought perhaps you really *were* falling for her."

"Tell me about that love affair of hers. How did the man get her to fall for him?"

"Believe it or not, by sheer indifference. Once he got her going, he pretended he didn't care whether she liked him or not. That bothered her. Men have always been the other way, threatening to kill themselves if she wouldn't marry them, and all that sort of stuff."

"You've talked with her?" I asked.

"Yes."

"About what happened?"

"Yes."

"Think she's telling the truth?"

"Yes. She heard the shot and looked at her watch the minute she got to her apartment."

"And she was cold sober?"

"She's always cold *and* sober."

I grinned at her and said, "I guess you've told me all I need to know, Rosalind. I won't have to waste time with Marilyn."

She said, "I've already given her the signal that you were falling for her and she's expecting to come over. Notice the way she's turning so you can see her curves? She'll look back at you over her shoulder in a minute, and give you a half smile. She got that pose from an art calendar."

I said, "It's a shame she's wasting it. Tell her I changed my mind, and decided she had halitosis or athlete's foot, or something. Good night."

"Will I be seeing you again?" she asked.

"That the standard line you hand all the customers?"

She looked at me frankly and said, "Sure. What the hell did you think? That I want to marry you? If you're a detective, be your age."

"Thanks," I told her. "You may see me again at that. In the meantime, I'm off."

"Where?"

"Leg work. *Lots* of leg work. Chores. Damn details. I hate them, but you have to do them."

She said, "I guess that's life. For you and me and the other guy."

"That the way it is with you?" I asked.

"Yes."

"Why?"

She made a little gesture and said, "Because I was a damn fool. I have to make a living. I've got a kid."

I said, "On second thought, I guess the information was worth ten dollars to the agency. Here's the other five."

"No kidding, it's on an expense account?"

"On an expense account—and my boss is a big-hearted egg."

Her hand joined mine. "Gosh, aren't you lucky—a boss like that!" The five-dollar bill slipped over into her palm. She walked with me as far as the door. "I like you," she said. "I wish you really *would* come back."

I nodded.

She said, "I tell all the customers that, but this time I happen to mean it."

I patted her shoulder and went on out. She stood in the door, watching me down the street. I caught a taxicab at the corner and drove out to the airport.

It was just the old routine leg work of a complete

check-up, but something you can't overlook if you want to be a good detective.

The passenger lists showed that Emory G. Hale had been a passenger on the 10:30 plane for New York City, that he'd returned on the plane, arriving at 8:30 that morning. I even checked to make sure he'd actually traveled on the plane.

The records showed that he had.

I took a cab back to the hotel. I was past due for a lot of shut-eye.

CHAPTER TWELVE

IT WAS PAST NOON when I went to Hale's apartment. He was out. I had a combined breakfast and lunch at the Bourbon House and tried Hale again.

No dice.

I went down St. Charles Avenue to the apartment house where Roberta had lived and studied the place as carefully as I could while walking by. Then I went back to the hotel and wrote out a typewritten report for the office files, being careful to list all my expenses.

I went back to the apartment at about four. Hale was in.

He was, moreover, in a very jovial mood.

"Come right in, Lam. Come in and sit down. Well, young man, I think I did you a little good. I drummed up another customer for you."

"That right?"

"Yes. A man was here asking about you. I gave you a very good recommendation, very good indeed."

"Thanks."

We sat looking at each other for a while; then he said, "It's very interesting. I've been searching the apartment."

"For what?"

"For something that might give us some clue."

"She hasn't lived here for three years."

"I know, but I was just looking around on the off chance. You can't tell when something might be found —letters or something."

"That's right."

"I've already found quite an assortment of things, letters that had worked under the papers that were placed on the bottom of the desk drawers, and there in the writing desk a whole lot of correspondence had dropped down in back of the drawer. I haven't got it all out yet. I put the drawer back when I heard your steps on the stairs. I didn't know just who it was that was coming."

He walked over to the desk and pulled out the top drawer.

"Don't happen to have a pocket flashlight, do you?" he asked.

"No."

He said, "I've been looking down here with a match, but it's rather dangerous. An end may drop off the match, and set the whole thing afire."

He struck a match, shielded the flame with his hand for a moment, then pushed his arm down inside the place where the drawer had been. "Take a look down there," he said.

Back down in the lower part of the desk I could see a litter of papers; then the match flickered out.

"Can't we get at them by taking the lower drawers out?" I asked.

"No. I've tried that. There's a partition back of the lower drawers. See?"

He pulled out one of the lower drawers. A solid partition was behind it. It left a space some six or eight inches between the back of the drawer and the back of the desk.

Hale said, "You see how it is. The upper drawer was made very deep so it would hold the desk blotter. The lower drawers aren't as deep by some eight inches. There was that much dead space in the desk."

I was curious now. "Not one chance in a hundred any of those papers concern the girl we want, but seeing we've gone this far, we may as well get them out."

"How?"

"We'll take everything out of the desk and stand the thing on its head."

Hale didn't say a word, started pulling the drawers out, and then removing things from the pigeonholes in the top of the desk, a bottle of ink, some pens, blotter, a couple of boxes of matches, and a few minor odds and ends which had accumulated as a hold-over from past tenants.

"Ready?" he demanded.

I nodded.

We each took hold of an end of the desk and moved it out from the wall.

Hale said, "I may as well confess to you, Lam, that I'm something of a detective myself. I'm interested in human nature, and nothing gives me quite as much pleasure as to be able to pry into the unexpected corners of the human mind. I like to read old correspondence. Came on a trunk full of letters at one time in connection with cleaning up an estate. Most interesting thing I've ever seen. Now, just tilt it down on that side. There we are. Easy now. Well, this trunk full of letters belonged to a woman who died at the age of seventy-eight. She'd saved every letter she'd ever received. Letters in there she'd received during her childhood, letters during the time she was being courted. Most interesting collection I've ever seen. And they weren't the repressed sort of letters that you'd expect either. Some of them were dynamite. Now, let's turn the thing right on over. Say, there's something heavy in there."

There was indeed something heavy in the desk. It slid down the back of the desk, lit against the inverted top with a thud, and then lodged there. We'd have to find some other way.

"Pick the desk up and shake it," I said. "Hold it down this way."

The desk was heavy. It took us a minute to get it elevated at just the right angle. When we had it sloped right, the heavy object thudded out to the floor. After that, I could hear the rustle of papers sliding out and dropping to the carpet. We couldn't see what they were while we were holding the desk.

"Give it a shake," I suggested.

We shook the desk. Hale took his big palm and pounded on the back. "I guess that's all."

We righted the desk and looked down at the pile of stuff on the floor. There were old letters, yellowed newspaper clippings, and the heavy object.

Hale and I stood staring at that heavy object.

It was a .38 caliber revolver.

I picked it up and looked at it. Four chambers of the cylinder were loaded. Two of them held exploded cartridges. There were some spots of rust on the gun, but, for the most part, it was in good condition.

Hale said, "Someone must have put that gun in the desk drawer on top of some papers, then as he opened the drawer hurriedly the gun dropped down behind and—"

"Wait a minute," I said. "Let's take a look at the way that drawer fits."

I fitted the drawer into the groove and looked at the space behind it.

"No dice," I told him. "That gun couldn't have dropped down behind there accidentally. The space is too small. That gun must have been deliberately dropped down there after someone had taken the drawer out. In other words, that was used, not as a place of storage but as a place of concealment."

Hale got down on his knees and struck two matches to verify my conclusions; then he said, "You're right, Lam! You really are a detective! Let's see what the letters have to say."

We picked up some of the old letters. They didn't mean much: some old receipted bills; a pleading, desperate letter from some woman who wanted a man to return and marry her; another letter from some man who wanted to borrow money to tide him him over an emergency and written in the "dear-old-pal" vein.

Hale chuckled. "I like these things," he said as he finished reading the letter. "Little cross-sections of life. Being perfect strangers to the transaction, we can examine the tone of that letter and see how badly that 'dear-old-pal' stuff is overdone. I wouldn't trust that man as far as I could throw this desk with one hand."

"Neither would I," I told him. "I wonder what the newspaper clippings are."

He pushed those to one side. "Those are meaningless. It's the letters that count. Here's one in feminine handwriting. Perhaps it's another letter from the girl who wanted the man to marry her. I wonder how *that* came out."

I picked up the old newspaper clippings, ran idly through them, said suddenly, "Wait a minute, Hale. We've struck something here."

"What?"

"Pay dirt."

"What do you mean?"

I said, "It may tie up with this thirty-eight caliber revolver."

Hale dropped the letter he was reading, said excitedly, "How's that?"

"These clippings have to do with the murder of a man by the name of Craig. Howard Chandler Craig. Twenty-nine years old, unmarried, employed as a bookkeeper by the Roxberry Estates. Let's see. Where was the murder committed? Wait a minute. Here's a heading. *Los Angeles Times, June 11, 1937.*"

Hale said, "Now wouldn't *that* be something? Suppose the murderer escaped and came here—" He picked up one of the clippings, started reading through it. It had been folded over a couple of times, and he unfolded it and looked at the photograph just about the time I was reading the details of the account.

When I heard Hale's quick intake of breath, I knew what caused it.

"Lam!" he said excitedly. "Look here!"

I said, "I'm reading about it in this one."

"But here's her photograph."

I looked at the coarse-meshed reproduction of Roberta Fenn's picture. Underneath it were the words *Roberta Fenn, twenty-one-year-old stenographer, was riding with Howard Craig when holdup occurred.*

Hale said excitedly, "Lam, do you know what this means?"

I said, "No."

He said, "I do."

"Don't be too sure you do. I don't."

"But it's as plain as the nose on your face."

I said, "Let's study these clippings before we go jumping to any hasty conclusions."

We read through all of the clippings, exchanging them with each other. Hale finished reading first.

"Well?" he asked when I'd finished.

I said, "Not necessarily."

"Bosh!" Hale said. "You can see it all as plain as day. She went out with this bookkeeper—probably another case of a girl wanting a man to marry her, and he refused. She got out of the car on some excuse or another, walked around to the driver's side, shot Craig twice through the left temple, hid the gun, and came in with this story of the masked bandit who had stepped out of the bush and ordered Craig to throw up his hands. He'd done it. The man had gone through his pockets, and then had ordered Roberta Fenn to walk down the road with him.

"That was more than Craig would stand for. He started the motor in his car, threw it into gear, and tried to run the man down, but the chap just managed to get to one side. He shot Craig twice in the head as the momentum of the car carried Craig up even with him.

"No one ever questioned the girl's story. Craig was considered a gentleman and a martyr. One reason police didn't question Roberta's story was that there had been two dozen petting-party holdups in the neighborhood within a period of a few months. On several occasions where the girl had been unusually attractive, the bandit had ordered her to walk down the road with him. There had been two other murders—"

Hale paused dramatically, motioned toward the gun, and said, "Well, there you are! It was murder. She got away with it once—and, by George, she tried getting away with it again. This time she can't make it stick."

I said, "Not necessarily. Simply because that's a thirty-eight caliber gun doesn't mean it's the same gun with which Craig was killed."

"Why are you protecting her?" Hale asked suspiciously.

"I don't know," I said. "Perhaps because I don't want you sticking your neck out."

"How do you mean?"

I said, "Making positive statements accusing a person of crime is sometimes dangerous, unless you have the information necessary to back them up."

Hale nodded. "That's so," he said. "Of course, there's nothing to *prove* that the gun goes with the newspaper clippings."

I pointed out, "The newspaper clippings could have been placed in that desk drawer, and worked on down through the opening in back. The gun couldn't. The gun was placed there deliberately."

Hale said, "Let me think."

I said, "While you're thinking, I'd better know exactly why you wanted Roberta Fenn, and who your client is."

"No. That doesn't enter into the picture."

"Why not?"

"Because I can tell you it doesn't. What's more, I'm protecting the confidence of my client."

"Don't you think that now he would want me to know more about it?"

"No."

"It's a man, isn't it—your client?"

"You can't pump me, Lam, and I don't want you to try. I told you I wanted you to find Roberta Fenn. That was all."

"Well, I've found her."

"And lost her again."

"That's one way of putting it."

He said, "Find her again."

"You haven't known Bertha very long, have you?"

"You mean Mrs. Cool?"

"Yes."

"No."

I said, "She's rather hard-boiled in a business deal."

"That's all right. I'm rather hard-boiled myself."

I said, "You employed the agency to find Roberta Fenn. You offered a bonus in the event she was found within a certain period of time."

"Well," he said impatiently, "what's wrong with that?"

I said, "We found her."

"But you didn't keep her found."

I said, "That's why I asked you if you'd had much experience with Bertha Cool. My best guess is that she'll say that all we were employed for was to find her."

"And that having found her, your employment is completed, and you're entitled to the bonus?"

"Exactly."

I waited for him to get mad. He didn't. He sat there on the floor, staring at the gun and the yellowed newspaper clippings. A smile twitched at the corners of his mouth; then the smile became a chuckle. "Damn it, Lam, she's right! Here I am, a lawyer, and I stick my neck out on an agreement of that sort."

He looked up at me.

I didn't say anything.

He said, "That is the agreement in a nutshell. I remember the way it was worded now." He laughed outright.

I said, "I thought I'd tell you, that's all."

"Well," he admitted, "that's one on me. Okay, I'll hire the firm all over again and arrange for another bonus. I like the way you work. In the meantime, we'd better get in touch with the police about this gun."

"What are you going to tell them?"

He said, "Don't worry, Lam. I'm going to tell them the bare facts, that I happened to be looking through the desk because I was interested in it as a piece of furniture. I intended to make the landlady an offer for it. I tilted it up in order to see the bottom, and realized there was something heavy in it. I shook it out, and the gun and these papers came out. Naturally, I don't want to appear in front of the public as a snoop who was going around reading correspondence that was really no concern of mine."

I said, "But you do want to get in touch with the police, is that it?"

"Yes, yes, of course."

I said, "Then the police will know as much about it as you do."

"Well, why not?"

I said, "I don't know anything about why you want Roberta Fenn or who wants her, but I suppose there's a reason."

He said, "Businessmen don't pay out good money to

find people just to ask them to subscribe to a magazine."

I said, "Perhaps you don't realize what I'm leading up to."

"Go ahead. Lead up to it."

"Let's suppose a businessman wants to find Roberta. He undoubtedly wants her to do something, or wants her to tell him something, or wants to find out something. Here's a thirty-eight caliber gun and some old newspaper clippings. You take those to the police, and you'll never find Roberta Fenn and get a chance to talk with her. That thing will be headlined all over the country. Right now the police think Roberta may have been a second victim, or they think she may have been frightened away. There's some speculation as to whether she might be the one who shot Nostrander, but she's not what you'd really call hot. Once you take this to the police, the police will reopen that old murder case. Then the California authorities will go crazy looking for her. You'll have both Louisiana and California police on her trail. You'll have her picture published in every newspaper in the country. You'll have posters made, and distributed in every post office, and mailed to every police officer in the land. Roberta will read all that stuff. She'll duck for cover. What sort of chance do you think *we* have of finding her ahead of the police of two states?

"When we do catch up with her she'll be in a cell. If you want her to do something, being in a cell might cramp her style."

He regarded me steadily for several seconds, his eyes batting every few seconds.

Abruptly he pushed the gun toward me. "All right, Lam, you take it."

"Not me. I'm simply a detective employed to find Roberta Fenn for a client whose identity I don't know. You're the big shot who's determining policies."

"Then," he said, "as an attorney in good standing, I would have no choice but to go to the police."

I got up from the floor and brushed my trousers. "Okay," I said, "I just wanted you to understand the situation."

I was halfway to the door before he called me back.

"Perhaps I should give the matter a little further consideration, Lam."

I didn't say anything.

He went on: "You know it's rather a serious matter to accuse a person of crime. I—er—I'll think it over."

I still didn't say anything.

"After all," he went on, "I'm *assuming* that this is the gun with which that crime in California was committed. That is pure inference on my part. I think it would be wise to make an investigation in greater detail. We really haven't anything to report to the police right now. We merely have found some newspaper clippings and a revolver concealed in an old desk. Thousands of people keep revolvers, and newspaper clippings are not necessarily significant."

"Done it?" I asked.

"Done what?"

"Convinced yourself that it's all right for you to do the thing you want to do."

"Hang it, Lam, I'm not doing that. I'm merely weighing the pros and cons."

"When you get them weighed, let me know," I told him, and turned once more toward the door.

This time he called me back before I had taken more than three steps.

"Lam."

I turned. "What is it this time?"

Hale was through beating around the bush. "Forget about this," he said. "We won't tell the police anything about it."

"What are you going to do with the gun?"

"Put it back in that desk just where we found it."

"Then what?"

"Later on, if it becomes necessary, we can discover it again."

I said, "You're the doctor."

He nodded and beamed at me. "The more I see of you, Lam, the more I appreciate you. Now I'd like to have you do something for me."

"What?"

"I understand the police have a witness who can fix the exact time Nostrander was murdered. One who heard the shots. A young woman, I believe."

"Yes."

"I wonder if it would be possible for you to arrange to have me meet her. Not in the capacity of a person seeking information, but merely casually."

I said, "It's all fixed. Be waiting out in front of the Jack-O'-Lantern Club about nine o'clock tonight. I've already paved the way."

"Well, well, *that's* efficiency! You seem to anticipate my every thought, Lam. You really do."

I said, "Nine o'clock tonight in front of the Jack-O'-Lantern," and went out.

I looked at my watch. It was two hours earlier in California. I sent a wire to the agency: *Howard Chandler Craig murdered June 6, 1937. Possibility of connection with case here. Get all details. In particular find out about habits and love life of victim.*

CHAPTER THIRTEEN

HALE SAID, "What a peculiar place."

"It's like all New Orleans nightclubs—that is, the ones in the French Quarter."

A waiter came over. "You want a table?"

I nodded.

We followed him over to the table he indicated and sat down. "Marilyn Winton works here?" Hale asked.

"Yes. She's the girl in the cream-colored satin."

"Marvelous figure," Hale commented appreciatively.

"Uh huh."

"I wonder if we could arrange to—well, you know, how are we going to get a chance to talk with her?"

"She'll be over."

"What makes you think so?"

"I have a hunch."

Marilyn had been in the game long enough so that when men's eyes started boring a hole in her back she turned instinctively.

She smiled; then she came over.

"Hello," she said to me.

I got up and said, "Hello. Marilyn, this is a friend of mine, Mr. Hale."

"Oh, how are you, Mr. Hale?" She gave him her hand.

Hale was standing up at his full height beaming down at her. The expression on his face was like that of a kid who is looking through a plate-glass store window at Santa Claus two days before Christmas.

"Won't you sit down?" I asked.

"Thanks."

We had no more than seated her when the waiter came up for an order.

"Plain water and whisky," she said.

"Gin and Coke," I ordered.

Hale pursed his lips thoughtfully. "Well, let me see. Do you have any real good cognac?"

I answered for the waiter. "No," I said. "Since you're here in New Orleans, why not drink a New Orleans drink? Gin and Seven-Up; gin and Coke; rum and Coke; or bourbon and Seven-Up?"

"Gin and Coke?" he inquired as though I'd suggested he try a chloride of lime cocktail. "Do you mean they mix them?"

"Bring him one," I told the waiter.

The waiter went away. Marilyn said to me, "Why did you run out on me—that other time?"

"Who said I did?"

"A little bird—and then I have eyes, you know."

"*I'll* say you have."

She laughed. "What's your name?"

"Donald."

"Next time don't get a girl all interested and then walk out."

Hale said to me, "You've talked with Miss Winton before?"

"No. I've wanted to, but—well, somehow, it just didn't come off."

She said, "Faint heart never won fair lady. Don't let things get you down, Donald."

The waiter brought our drinks. Hale paid for them. He picked his glass up, an expression of austere disapproval held in escrow on his face, ready to be delivered as soon as the first sip of liquid passed over his tongue. I saw a look of surprise on his face; then he took another sip and said, "Good heavens, Lam, that's *good!*"

"I told you it was."

"Why, I like it. It's a delightful drink. Much better than the conventional Scotch and soda. It has just enough body without having a cloying sweetness."

Marilyn sipped her cold tea and said, "I like this bourbon and plain water. It's a nice drink—when you're doing quite a bit of drinking."

Hale seemed shocked. He looked her over and said, "Do *you* do a lot of drinking?"

"Oh, off and on."

His eyes looked her over, searching for evidences of extreme dissipation.

"Cigarette?" I asked her.

"Please."

I gave her a cigarette. Hale took a cigar. We lit up.

"Where are you boys from?" she asked.

I said, "My friend's from New York."

"Must be quite a city. I've never been there. I think I'd be afraid to go."

"Why?" Hale asked her.

"Oh, I don't know. Big cities terrify me. I know I couldn't find my way around."

Hale contrived to cast himself in the role of cosmopolite by saying, "I think New York is an easy city to get around in. Chicago and Saint Louis are much more difficult."

"They're all too big for me."

"If you ever come to New York, let me know, and I'll see that you don't get lost."

"Or stolen?" she asked, her eyes laughing.

"Yes."

"How about strayed?"

"Well," Hale deliberated, and glanced at me. A smirk began forming about the corners of his mouth. "If you stay with me, you won't stray very far."

"No-o-o-o?" she asked with just the right rising inflection, using her eyes.

Hale laughed as though he'd received a shot of vitamins. "I like this drink, Lam. I like it very much. I'm certainly glad you called my attention to it. I like this New Orleans type of nightclub, so cosy, so intimate, so typical of the French Quarter. There's a certain distinctive, informal atmosphere which you wouldn't find anywhere else, eh?"

I grinned across at Marilyn and said, "I'll give you one guess as to who's having a good time."

"I don't think *you* are."

"What makes you think so?"

"You haven't said so."

"I'm the strong, silent type!"

Rosalind walked by. Marilyn looked at her as a watchdog might look at a tramp. Rosalind gave me no sign. Marilyn looked away, and I got a quick, intimate, split-second smile; then her face was a dead blank once more.

I ground out my cigarette in the ash tray, dropped my hand to my coat pocket, and surreptitiously dumped all of the cigarettes except one out of the package.

Hale said, "I think this is one of the most delightful drinks I've ever tasted."

Marilyn tossed off the rest of her cold tea, said, "If you take two or three of them one right after the other, you really feel good. But you never get high on them, just a pleasant glow."

"Is that so?"

She nodded.

"I like to sip a drink like this," Hale said.

I said, "Be a sport and drink it down. Marilyn wants us to buy another drink."

Her eyes caressed me. "How did you know?"

"I'm psychic."

"I believe you are." Her hand came across the table to rest on mine.

The psychic one was the waiter. He materialized by the table without any apparent signal.

"Fill them up again," I said.

I took the cigarette package from my pocket, extended it to Marilyn. "How about another one?"

"Thanks."

She took it, and I fumbled around in the package with my forefinger.

"I believe I took the last one," she said.

I shook the package, grinned, crushed it, said, "That's all right. I'll get more."

"The waiter will bring some."

"No. This is fine, thanks. I see a machine over there."

I held a match to her cigarette, shook it out, got up, and walked over to the cigarette-vending machine. I pretended I was out of change, and went over to the bar to get some. After getting the package of cigarettes, I paused by the pinball machine and played a game. While I was doing that I slid my right hand down into my coat pocket, got hold of the discarded cigarettes I'd slipped out from the other package, crumbled them into a ball, and dropped them unobtrusively on the floor.

I finished my game on the pinball machine and managed to ring up a couple of free games.

I looked back over at the table. Marilyn was watching me, but Hale was leaning forward, pouring conversation into her ear. The three new drinks were on the table.

I waved my hand, called out, "This is velvet," and turned back to the pinball machine.

Rosalind walked up to the cigarette-vending machine, fumbled in her purse for coins, said out of the corner of her mouth, "Don't look up."

I kept playing the pinball machine.

"Don't make any play for me. It would cost me my job. She's interested in you. When you walked out on her, it knocked her for a loop. But—don't go overboard."

"Why?"

"You'd be sorry."

"Thanks."

She picked up her cigarettes and turned away.

I swung around so I could see the mirror over the bar. Marilyn was watching her with the cold, unwinking stare of a snake regarding a young bird that has just fluttered to the ground.

I kept on shooting balls in the machine, used up my two free games, started feeding in coins.

Hale was really going to town. He'd worked up a lot of enthusiasm now, making gestures with his hands, looking in Marilyn's eyes, occasionally letting his glance stray down to the bare shoulders.

I went back to the table.

Emory Hale was saying, "—exceedingly fascinating."

Marilyn was giving him the steady eye. She said, "I'm

102

glad you think so because I find mature people so *much* more interesting than the men of my own age. Somehow those younger men can't seem to hold my attention. After a little while they bore me to distraction. Now why is that, Emory? Is there something wrong with me?"

He beamed across at her. At that particular moment he didn't know I was anywhere in the country and she couldn't see me without turning.

"Go on," she pleaded. "If you know why it is, tell me."

I cleared my throat. Neither of them looked up.

He said, "It's because, my dear, you have such a fine mind. You can't be interested in the mediocre banalities of adolescent conversation. Despite your beautiful body and your very evident youth, it's quite apparent that you—"

I backed up a few steps, coughed loudly, and came walking toward the table.

Marilyn said, "We thought we'd lost you."

"I went to buy some cigarettes."

"I'll take one," she said.

Hale kept looking at her while I opened the package.

"How's the pinball machine?" Marilyn asked.

"Pretty fair. I won a few."

"Cash in?"

"No. Played back."

"I always do that. They say it's foolish. You should cash in your winnings."

"I can't see that it makes much difference."

"If you don't cash them in, the machine eventually cleans you."

"It does anyway."

She thought that over.

Emory Hale cleared his throat. "As I was saying, it is very seldom that one finds a mind capable of developing the mature outlook before—"

She said, "Oh, *there's* the waiter—looking over this

way. I guess he sees my glass is empty. He's such a funny chap. Do you know if I sit here with an empty glass, he'll stand there and stare at us as though he was trying to hypnotize me. Why, you have a drink there which you haven't touched, Donald."

I said, "That's right. I should have taken it over to the pinball machine with me. Well, here's happy days."

"But I have nothing to drink with."

"We'll have to remedy that."

Hale said, "I think you have the most wonderful hair."

"Thanks. . . . Joe, I'll have another whisky and water."

The waiter turned to Hale.

"Bring him another Coke and gin," I said. "Fix it so he can taste it if you don't want the party to go dead."

The waiter looked at Hale, then looked at me. "Okay, what do you want?"

"This is a hold-over. I'm keeping it."

He said, "You're entitled to another drink at no extra charge. When you have a girl at the table, you—"

"I know all about that," I told him. "Get these drinks before these people die of thirst in the middle of your night spot."

Marilyn laughed at that.

Hale started rubbering around the room.

Marilyn took a deep drag at her cigarette and said casually, "You'll find it through the archway in that next room."

Hale seemed embarrassed. "I beg pardon."

"That's where it is."

"What?"

"What you're looking for."

Hale cleared his throat, pushed back his chair, said with dignity, "Excuse me for a moment."

"Guess he can't take it too well," I said, as she watched him cross the room.

"A lot of those old bozos can't. He's a nice guy, isn't he, Donald?"

She was watching me intently.

"Uh huh."

"You don't seem to put much enthusiasm in it."

"What do you want me to do? Stand at attention or jump up on the table and start waving a flag?"

"Don't be silly. I just said he was a good guy."

"Don't be silly, yourself. I said he was, too."

She looked down at the table for a while, then suddenly looked back up at me and smiled, that steady-eyed, direct smile which had such a suggestion of intimacy. "Don't get me wrong, Donald. I mean that he's a good enough guy, but—well, you know how it is. Youth appeals to youth and—"

"Go ahead," I said, "finish it," as she seemed to stall on dead center. "What does age appeal to?"

"Nothing."

I laughed.

"It's the God's truth. The old women want young men, and the old men want the flappers. If the older men would give the older women just a little attention, it would make everybody a lot happier." She kept her eyes on mine. "As for me, *I* want youth."

She put her hand across the table and squeezed mine. "What did you say to that girl?"

"What girl?"

"The one who came over to use the cigarette machine when you were playing the pinball machine—Rosalind. You bought her a drink when you were here before—remember?"

I said, "I didn't place her at first. I guess she's sore. I kept looking at you when she was with me. She noticed it. I think it made her mad."

"Oh."

"Aren't you and Emory getting along?" I asked.

"Oh, yes. Famously. Why?"

"I was wondering after what you said about older men and wanting youth."

She smiled and said, "Oh, in a way *he's* different. He's so quaint and—sort of old-fashioned. He's like a father to me. What does he do?"

"He's a New York lawyer."

"Oh, a lawyer! Successful?"

I said, "He's got money to burn. And he isn't one of the hard-boiled kind that know all the tricks. He specializes on probate work. He's really a babe in the woods."

She said, "It's funny, but I thought there was something in his life—oh, you know what I mean. An aura of misfortune that clings to him. Perhaps he's unhappily married. That may be it. Domestic troubles."

"I don't think there's anything to that theory. I gathered the impression he's a wealthy widower."

"Oh."

I said, "Here he comes now. Look at the way he's walking. He's certainly picking them up and putting them down carefully."

She laughed and said, "Another gin and Coke and his feet won't even touch the floor. Look, Donald," she said hurriedly, "you know that girl I was talking to you about?"

"You mean Rosalind?"

"Yes."

"What about her?"

"Try and find an opportunity to speak to her. She's just absolutely crazy about you, simply nuts. Perhaps you don't realize it, but when a girl in a place like this falls for a man the way she does for you, it hurts her terribly to have you come in and sit with another girl. *Do* try and say something nice to her, won't you?"

"Why, sure. I didn't think she even remembered me."

"Remember you! I tell you she's crazy about you. . . . Oh, you're back, Emory? Just in time for your drink. Joe's bringing one over. How do you feel?"

Hale said, "Like a million dollars."

Marilyn said, "There's Rosalind now. Rosalind's a great one for the pinball machine. I'll bet she keeps herself broke playing the pinball. During the daytime when business is slack, you know."

Marilyn looked significantly at me and smiled.

"Excuse me," I said.

I got up and wandered over to the pinball machine. Out of the corner of my eye I saw Marilyn give Rosalind a signal.

I'd shot the third ball on the machine when I noticed Rosalind standing beside me. "What did you do to her?" she asked.

"Why?"

"She gave me the highball to pick you up."

I said, "I let her think she had a diamond-studded live one."

"Is he?"

"Maybe."

"Friend of yours?"

"In a way. Why?"

"Nothing. I was just wondering."

I finished out the game on the pinball machine, fed a coin in the slot, and pushed in the plunger. "Want to try it?" I asked.

She started shooting balls around the board. Joe came over and looked at me significantly.

"Couple of drinks," I ordered.

"What's yours?" he asked Rosalind.

"Same old stuff. This guy is wise to the joint, Joe. Don't bother with the hooey. Just bring me the cold tea. You'll get the dough."

"Yours?" Joe asked me, grinning.

"Gin and Seven-Up."

Rosalind and I finished our drinks at the pinball machine. "You going back?" she asked.

"Perhaps."

"Marilyn wants me to stay with you."

"Why not? Come on over and meet Emory."

"You aren't sore, are you?"

"At what?"

"Oh—Marilyn. You don't—you didn't really fall for her, did you?"

I grinned at her. "Come on over. Sit down and join the party."

She said, "You did a swell job with Marilyn."

"Why?"

"She was looking daggers at me a few minutes ago when she thought I was making a play for you. Now she's signaled me to go ahead."

"Circumstances alter cases."

She said, "Donald, you're a deep one. Just *what* are you after?"

"Nothing that's going to hurt you any."

She looked at me and said, "I'll bet you'd give a girl a square deal at that."

I didn't say anything. We walked over to the table.

Marilyn said casually, "Oh, hello, Rosalind. This is Emory, my friend, Mr. Emory—Smith."

She turned to Hale and flashed him a quick wink.

Rosalind said, "How do you do, Mr. Smith?"

Hale got up and bowed. I held a chair for Rosalind. We sat down.

Marilyn said to Hale, "I don't like to talk about it. Let's talk about something else."

"What don't you like to talk about?" I asked.

Hale said, "What happened this morning."

"What happened?"

"Marilyn heard the shot that killed that lawyer. You remember reading about it in the papers?"

I said, "Oh."

"She was coming in around three o'clock in the morning," Hale said.

"Two-thirty," Marilyn corrected.

Hale frowned. "Why, I thought you told me it was somewhere between two-thirty and three."

"No. I looked at my watch. It must have happened just a second or two after two-thirty."

"Wrist watch?" Hale asked.

"Yes."

He reached across the table, took her wrist in his hand, and looked at the diamond-studded watch.

"My, what a beauty!"

"Isn't it?"

"I'll bet someone thought a lot of you to give you that. May I look at it?"

She unsnapped it, and Hale turned it over and over in his fingers. "A very beautiful watch," he said, "very, very beautiful."

I said to Rosalind, "What is there to do in this place? Don't they dance?"

"No. They have a floor show."

"When?"

"It'll be on almost any minute now."

Marilyn laughed and said, "There's Joe looking at your empty glass, Rosalind."

Hale said, "Just a minute, and he can look at mine." He tossed down the rest of his drink, snapped his fingers, and said, "Oh, Joe."

The waiter didn't waste any time this trip. "Fill 'em up with the same thing?" he asked.

"Fill 'em up same thing," Hale said, still fingering Marilyn's wrist watch.

Joe brought the drinks. The lights dimmed. Marilyn said, "This is the floor show coming on. You'll love it."

Chairs scraped over the floor as a girl with an Egyptian profile, a pair of shorts covered with hieroglyphics, and a bra decorated in the same way came out, sat cross-legged on the floor, and made angles with her hands and elbows. She got a spattering of applause. A man with boisterous hilarity came out and made a few off-color cracks into a microphone. A strip-tease artist did her stuff, finishing up in the middle of a blue spot that furnished all the clothing. She got a terrific hand. Then the Egyptian dancer came back into the blue spot wearing a grass skirt with a lei around her neck and an imitation hibiscus in her hair. The bird who had put on the monologue played a uke, and she did her version of the hula.

When the lights came up again, Hale handed Marilyn the wrist watch he'd been playing with during the floor show.

"That all of it?" I asked Rosalind.

Marilyn said, "No. It's just an intermission. There'll be another act in a minute or two. This gives us a chance to get our glasses filled up."

Joe filled up our glasses.

Hale grinned across the table at me, the man-of-the-world grin. "Havin' a swell time," he said. "Bes' little girl in the world. Bes' drinks in the world. Gonna have all my friends in when I get back t' New York, show 'em fine New Orleans drinks. Makes you feel good. Don't get drunk. Jus' get to feeling good."

"That's right," I told him.

Marilyn put the wrist watch back on. A second or two later she was looking at me, then at Rosalind. She wiped her wrist with a napkin, said, "Ain't we got fun?"

The second act started. The man who had been playing the uke came out in evening clothes and put on a series of dances with the Egyptian dancer; then the strip-tease artist did a fan dance. The lights went back up, and Joe was at our elbows.

"How many Joes are there?" I asked Marilyn.

"Just one. Why?"

"He seems to be twins."

"You seein' two of 'em?" Hale asked solicitously.

I said, "No. I only *see* one, but the other one is over at the bar getting the drinks mixed. He'll come back with the drinks while this one is over at the bar getting more drinks mixed. One man couldn't make that many round trips."

Joe looked down at me with the half smile on his lips,

an expression of detached amusement, not unmixed with contempt.

Hale started to laugh. His laughter kept getting louder. I thought he was going to fall off the chair.

Marilyn waved her hand. "Same thing all around."

Abruptly I pushed back my chair. "I'm going home," I said.

Rosalind looked at me. "Aw, gee, Donald, you just got here."

I took her hand, held it in mine long enough to slip her a couple of folded dollar bills. "I'm sorry. I'm not feeling good. That last drink didn't agree with me."

Hale laughed uproariously. "Ought to drink gin and Coke," he said. "That stuff you can drink all night. Marvelous drink. Makes you feel good, but doesn't get you tight. You youngsters can't stand anything. We know, don't we, Marilyn?"

He looked across at her with a loose-lipped leer, his alcohol-lighted eyes peering out from over the folds of flushed skin.

Marilyn put her hand across to let it rest on his for a moment. A little later she freed her hand, moistened the tip of her napkin in the water glass, and rubbed it on her wrist.

I said, "Good night, everybody."

Hale peered up at me. For a moment the laughter left his face. He started to say something, then changed his mind, turned back to Marilyn, thought of something else, swung around to me, and said, "This is a smart bird, Marilyn. You wanna watch him."

"What kind of a bird?" she asked—"not a pigeon!"

"No," Hale said, failing to get the significance of her remark. "He's an owl—you know—wise guy. Always said he was 'n owl."

That idea struck him as funny. When I went out of the door he was laughing so hard he could hardly catch his breath. Tears were beginning to trickle down his cheeks.

I got to the hotel. Bertha had arrived in Los Angeles. There was the characteristic wire from her: *What's the idea digging in last year's rabbit warren? We are too short-handed to scare up dope on old murder cases. Felonies outlaw in this state after three years. What sort of a bird do you think you are?*

I went down to the telegraph office and was feeling just good enough to send her the reply I wanted: *Murder never outlaws. Hale says I'm an owl.*

I sent the message collect.

CHAPTER FOURTEEN

I GOT UP AT SEVEN O'CLOCK, showered, shaved, had breakfast, and unpacked my bag to dig out the revolver that I was supposed to carry. It was a .38, blued steel, in only fair condition. I put it in my pocket and walked down Royal Street to the entrance to the apartment. I wondered how much of a hangover Hale had.

I didn't try to be quiet as I climbed the stairs. I made noise, lots of it, and my knock on the door wasn't at all gentle.

Hale didn't answer.

I started both knuckles to work and used the toe of my shoe to give the summons a little more interest.

Still no Hale.

I had the extra key to the apartment. I fitted this key to the lock and clicked back the bolt.

Hale wasn't there.

The bed was rumpled, but the wrinkles in the sheet didn't look as though it had been slept in much longer than an hour.

I walked across the bedroom into the living-room,

looked out onto the porch to make certain he wasn't there. Assured that the coast was clear, I took the drawers out of the writing-desk, tilted it up on one corner, and spilled out the debris from the bottom: letters, clippings, and the gun.

I pocketed the gun that had been in there, replaced it with my own revolver, and then put the desk back into shape.

It was a fine warm day, and the street below was filling up with people who were strolling around, enjoying the sunlight.

I gave the place a final once-over, then quietly opened the door, pulled it shut behind me, and went down the stairs.

I was in the courtyard when I met the colored maid. She gave me a grin and said, "Is the ge'man up yet?"

I assured her that the "ge'man" was either out or was asleep, that I'd pounded on the door, and hadn't been able to raise him.

She thanked me and went on up.

I went back to the hotel. There was a memo in my box to call Lockley 9746.

I went into a booth and called the number, wondering whether it would be a hospital or the jail. It was neither. A velvet feminine voice answered the telephone.

"Someone calling Mr. Lam?"

She laughed. "Oh, yes. This is the office of the Silkwear Importation Company calling its president."

"Indeed."

"You have a letter and a telegram here."

"Business is picking up," I said.

"Isn't it! Know what happened? Listen to this. We send out two form letters, one by air mail, and we get two replies back, one of them by wire."

"That's the way to write sales letters," I said.

"It was on account of the excellent job of mimeographing," she retorted.

"I'll take your word for it and be right up."

I took a cab up to the office. Ethel Wells seemed really glad to see me. "How's everything this morning?" she asked.

"Not so hot."

"No? What's wrong?"

"I started out last night to show a tourist the town."

"You look as fresh as a daisy."

"I feel as though someone had pulled my petals off to see whether she loves me or loves me not."

"Don't feel badly about it. Perhaps the answer was that she really loves you."

I didn't have any answer for that, so I tore open the telegram.

It read: *Silkwear Importation Company. Send five dozen pair express collect size ten and one-half, color four your chart.*

The telegram was signed, *Bertha Cool,* and the address given was that of the agency.

The letter was in a tinted square envelope. The stationery inside matched it. There was a faint scent. The postmark on the envelope was *Shreveport, Louisiana.* The letter bore the date line, *Shreveport.* It read simply, *Send me six pair of your hose; size eight and one-half, color number five according to your chart.*

The letter was signed *Edna Cutler,* and there was a street address.

I put the letter in my pocket, said to Ethel Wells. "When would I be able to get a train for Shreveport?"

"Must it be a train?"

"A bus will do all right."

She reached into a cubbyhole beneath the counter which ran on one side of her desk, pulled out a bus schedule, opened it, and handed it to me.

"I see where I made my mistake," she said.

"What?"

"I should have ordered *my* stockings by mail and given *my* home address."

"Why don't you try it?" I asked.

She was holding her lead pencil in her right hand, making aimless little diagrams across the page of her shorthand notebook.

She said, very demurely, "I think I will."

I handed her the bus schedule. "I'll be out of town today, Miss Wells," I said very importantly. "If anyone wants to see me, I'm in conference."

"Yes, sir. And if any more letters come in, what shall I do?"

"There won't be any more."

"You wouldn't want to bet on it, would you?"

"I might."

"A pair of silk stockings?"

"Against what?"

"Anything you want. I'm betting on a cinch."

I said, "It's a bet. I want to see what's in the letter. I have to have a residence address, you know, or I can't fill orders."

She smiled. "I know. Watch your step in Shreveport."

CHAPTER FIFTEEN

IT WAS AROUND EIGHT O'CLOCK in the evening when I rang the buzzer on the apartment at the address given me in Edna Cutler's letter.

A feminine voice came drifting down through the little telephone set. "Who is it, please?"

I placed the transmitter to my lips. "A representative of the Silkwear Importation Company."

"I thought you were in New Orleans."

"We have branches all over the country—special field representatives."

115

"Couldn't you come tomorrow?"

"No. I'm making a swing through this section of the state."

"Well, I can't see you tonight."

"Sorry," I said in a tone of finality.

"Wait a minute. When *can* I see you?"

"When I make my next trip through here."

"When will that be?"

"Three or four months."

There was an exclamation of dismay. "Oh, hang it—I'm dressing. Wait a minute. I'll throw something on and open the door. Come on up."

The buzzer sounded, and I climbed a flight of stairs and walked down a long corridor, looking at door numbers.

Edna Cutler, attired in a blue dressing-gown, stood in the doorway waiting for me. She said, "I thought you shipped by mail."

"We do."

"Well, come on in. Let's get it over with. Why did you come personally?"

I said, "We have to conform with the regulations of the F.I.C."

"What's the F.I.C.?"

"Federal Importing Commission."

"Oh. I don't see why."

I smiled and said, "My dear young woman, we'd be subject to a fine of ten thousand dollars and imprisonment for twelve months if we sold to other than private individuals. We aren't allowed to sell to any dealers, or to any person who intends to resell our merchandise."

"I see," she said, somewhat mollified.

She was dark, although not so dark as Roberta Fenn. She was expensive. Her hair, her eyebrows, the curl of her long lashes, the enamel on her nails showed the sort of care which costs both time and money. Women lavish that type of care on themselves only when they are prop-

116

erty which is well worth the investment. I looked her over carefully.

"Well?" she asked, smiling tolerantly as she noticed the excursions made by my eyes.

I said, "You still haven't convinced me."

"*I* haven't convinced *you?*"

She looked like a young woman who knew her way around. Sitting there in her apartment wearing a negligee, which showed enough bare leg to demonstrate clearly that she was entitled to an AAA1 priority on stockings, she was neither forward nor in the slightest degree embarrassed. So far as she was concerned, I wasn't a human being. I was simply six pair of stockings at a bargain price.

"I'll want to see samples," she observed abruptly.

"The guarantee protects you."

"How do I know it does?"

"Because you don't pay anything until you've not only received the stockings, but have worn them for a full thirty days."

She said, "I shouldn't think you could afford to do that."

"The only way we can is by having a very select mailing list. However, we want to get down to business. I have half a dozen other calls to make. Your name's Edna Cutler. You want these stockings exclusively for your own use?"

"Yes, of course."

"Now, I understand that you aren't in business. I'm taking your assurance that none of these stockings will be offered for sale again?"

"Why, certainly. I want them for myself."

"And perhaps some friends?"

"What's that got to do with it?"

"We'd have to have the names of the friends. That's the only way we can keep our import permit from the Federal government."

She studied me curiously. "That sounds just a little fishy to me."

I laughed and said, "You should try doing business now—even an ordinary business is bad enough. But try doing something where you have to import merchandise from a foreign country and see what happens."

"How did you get hold of these stockings down in Mexico?"

I laughed. "That's a secret."

"I think I'd like to find out more about it just the same."

I said, "A Japanese ship was carrying a load of hosiery. The Japs raided Pearl Harbor. The ship, like nearly all Japanese ships, was intended for commerce in time of peace, but in time of war it had a certain military mission to perform. The captain put ashore in Mexico on the coast of Lower California, picked a sandy place, dug a long trench, and buried the bulk of the silk goods from his hold. My partner happened to own the tract of land where the stuff was buried. He also happened to have some pull in Mexico City. As a result—well, you can gather—"

She said, "You mean this stuff is highjacked?"

"The Supreme Court of Mexico has given us title to it. We can get you a copy of the decision if you want."

"But if you have any quantity of silk goods that you received under circumstances such as that, why don't you bring them up, take them across the border, then sell them to some of the big department stores and—"

I explained patiently, "We can't do that. Under our license with the government, we have to sell the stockings to individual customers."

"Your letter didn't say so."

"No. It's a ruling of the F.I.C. We couldn't bring them into the country otherwise."

I took a pencil and notebook from my pocket. "Now if you'll kindly give me the names of any intimate friends to whom you'll deliver any of these—"

"I want those stockings for my own use. However, I might refer you to a friend who'd take some."

"That would be fine. Now did you—"

The door from the bedroom opened, and Roberta Fenn came breezing into the room. She'd evidently just finished dressing.

"Hello," she said. "Are you the stocking man? I was just telling my friend that—"

She stood perfectly still. Her eyes widened, her mouth fell slightly open.

Edna Cutler whirled around quickly, caught the expression on her face, jumped to her feet with alarm, and cried, "Why, Rob, what's the matter?"

"Nothing," Roberta Fenn said after taking a deep breath. "He's a detective, Edna, that's all."

Edna Cutler whirled back to me with indignation and perhaps a trace of fear in her manner. It was the instinctive fight which a frightened animal puts up when it's driven into a corner.

"How dare you come in here in this way? I could have you arrested."

"And I could have you arrested for sheltering a person who's accused of murder."

The two women exchanged glances. Roberta said, "I think he's really clever, Edna. I don't think we're going to get anywhere with that approach."

She sat down.

Edna Cutler hesitated for a long moment; then she, too, sat down.

Roberta said, "It was a clever trick all right. Edna and I wondered how anyone had got that address; then we decided that the post office probably took addresses from letters and sold mailing lists."

I said, "No need to talk about that. That's water over the dam."

"It was a *clever* trick," Roberta repeated, glancing significantly at Edna Cutler.

I said, "Any one of half a dozen tricks would have accomplished the same purpose. If I found you, the police can find you. The wonder of it is they haven't found you sooner."

Roberta said, "I don't think the police will find me. I think you underestimate your own abilities."

I said, "We won't argue about it. We have other things to discuss. Who was Paul Nostrander?"

They exchanged glances.

I looked at my wrist watch. "We haven't much time to waste."

Edna Cutler said, "I don't know."

I looked at Roberta, and her eyes avoided mine.

I turned back to Edna Cutler. "Suppose I refresh your recollection a bit. You were married to Marco Cutler. He wanted to file suit for divorce. You didn't want to let him go without more alimony than he was willing to pay. Unfortunately, however, you'd been indiscreet."

"That's a lie."

I said, "Well, let's put it this way. He had witnesses who would *swear* that you had been indiscreet."

"And *they* were lying!"

I said, "Forget it. I don't care about the merits or demerits of that divorce action. I don't care if Marco Cutler had perjured witnesses, or whether circumstantial evidence looked black against you, or whether he could have named seventy-five corespondents and still missed a couple of dozen. What I'm getting at, and want to establish definitely, is that he wanted to get a divorce, that you didn't want him to get a divorce, and that you didn't have any defense."

She said, "Put it that way then, and go on from there, I'm not admitting anything. I'm not denying anything. I'm listening."

I said, "The stunt you pulled was a masterpiece."

"If you're so smart, tell me the rest of it."

I said, "You went to New Orleans. You let your husband know you were in New Orleans. You let him believe that you had run out of California because you didn't want the notoriety of having the things you had done dragged into the limelight. Marco Cutler thought it was all cut and dried. You'd played right into his hands. He'd been very smart. You'd been very dumb. He wasn't going to pay you a cent of alimony.

"There's where you pulled your fast one. You let him know that you were taking an apartment. You gave him the address. Then you looked around for someone who had a superficial resemblance to you; height, size, age, and in a general way, complexion. Anyone seeing you and Roberta Fenn together wouldn't think there was much similarity, but a written description of one of you could well be taken as a description of the other."

Edna Cutler said, "If you're getting ready to say something, go ahead and say it."

"I'm simply laying the foundation."

"Well, go ahead with the superstructure. We haven't all night. You yourself said you were in a hurry."

I said, "I believe my words were that there wasn't any time to waste. If you think I'm wasting it, you're crazy."

Roberta Fenn smiled.

"Go ahead," Edna Cutler challenged.

"You found Roberta Fenn. She was very much on the loose. You had a little money. You wanted to give her your apartment rent free. Perhaps you offered to pay her something in addition. The only condition you made was that she was to keep your name, receive your mail, forward it on to you, and tell anyone who asked that she was Edna Cutler. You *may* have told her you expected papers to be served on you in a divorce suit. Perhaps you didn't.

"In any event, your husband walked into the trap. He went to his lawyers. He told them all about the cause of action he had, and the lawyers suggested that they file a complaint which just stated facts sufficient to constitute a cause of action. Then if you started fighting, they'd amend the complaint and drag in all the dirt. They asked your husband where you were, and he gave them the address in New Orleans. The lawyers, steeped in the legal lore of the profession, concentrated all their attention on working the old trick of filing a relatively innocuous complaint, but letting you know that if you tried to protect yourself, they'd come down on you with an avalanche of mud."

The mere mention of it made Edna's eyes glitter. "And you think that was fair?"

"No. It's a lousy trick. It's one that lawyers work all the time."

"The effect of it was to deprive me of any opportunity to fight for my rights."

"You should have gone ahead and fought, anyway—if you had anything to fight for."

"I was framed."

"I know," I said, "but we're not trying the divorce case on the merits. I'm just sketching a picture of what happened. The lawyers sent the papers to a New Orleans process server. The process server came lumbering up the steps, pounded on the door, looked Roberta over, said, 'You're Edna Cutler,' and handed her papers. He made a return of service that he'd duly and regularly served Edna Cutler on a certain day and date in New Orleans. You, of course, were far, far away."

Edna said, "You're making it sound like a conspiracy. As a matter of fact, I didn't know anything whatever about the divorce until very recently."

I turned my eyes to Roberta. "That was because you didn't know where to notify her?"

She nodded.

"It was very, very clever," I said. "It's a very neat way of turning defeat into triumph. Marco Cutler thought he had a good divorce. He went to Mexico before he had a final decree, and remarried. You waited long enough so it would look as though you were acting in good faith. Then you wrote Roberta Fenn a letter, asking her to be nice to some man who was a friend of yours. That was the first time Roberta had had your address. She answered that letter by writing to tell you that after you had left, papers had been served on her, that because she had promised you that no matter what happened, she'd swear she was Edna Cutler, she had told the man who served the papers that that was her name. You immediately wrote back and asked Roberta to send the papers on to you. She sent them on, and that gave you all you needed to swear that that was the first time you had any knowledge you had been divorced. Prior to that time you thought you were still the wife of Marco Cutler, separated, of course, but still his wife.

"So you wrote to your husband and asked him how he got that way, pointing out to him that his divorce wasn't any good because the papers hadn't been served on you. In other words, you now had him hooked, and you were going to make him pay through the nose. He didn't dare let his present wife get the least inkling of the true facts of the case. In short, you've got him where you want him."

I quit talking and looked at her, waiting for her to say something.

At length, she said, "*You* make it sound as though I had worked it out as a clever idea. As a matter of fact, I had absolutely no thought of anything except to get away from it all. My husband had framed me. He had subjected me to all sorts of humiliations. I don't know whether it was because he had determined to smear me so badly I couldn't hold my head up among my friends, or whether he himself had been victimized. He'd hired private detectives and had paid them a fancy sum. Those detectives had to produce evidence to get money, so they kept sending in all sorts of lies to Marco, and Marco gleefully thought he was getting something on me. He paid them fabulous sums."

She stopped for a moment and bit her lip, apparently fighting for self-control.

"And then?" I asked.

"Then," she said, "when he told me what he had,

when he showed me the reports of the detective agency, when he let me read that pack of lies, I almost went crazy."

"You didn't admit them, did you?"

"Admit them! I told him they were the most awful lies I had ever read anywhere. I had a complete nervous breakdown. I was under the care of a physician for two weeks, and it was my doctor who told me to travel and get away from everything, to go some place where there would be nothing to remind me of what had happened, simply to clear out."

"A sympathetic doctor?" I asked, smiling.

"He was very understanding."

"Gave you his advice in writing?" I asked.

"How did you know?"

"I was just wondering."

"Well, as a matter of fact, he did. I went to San Francisco. While I was there, I wrote him a letter. I told him I didn't feel like coming back and asked him what he thought I should do, and he wrote me this letter telling me he thought it was an excellent idea for me to get a complete change."

"And, of course, you just happen to have saved that letter. Go ahead."

"I went to New Orleans. Everything was fine for about three weeks. I stayed in a hotel, while I was looking around to find an apartment. Then something happened."

"What was it?"

"I met someone on the street."

"Someone who knew you?"

"Yes."

"From Los Angeles?"

"Yes. So I decided to disappear."

I said, "That doesn't work. If you met someone on the street in New Orleans who knew you in Los Angeles, you'd also meet someone on the street in Little Rock, Arkansas, Shreveport, or Timbuctoo."

"No. You don't get it. The friend wanted to know where I was living. I had to tell her. I knew that she'd tell her friends, and the first thing I knew, everybody would know that I was in New Orleans, and be looking me up. I didn't want to see people who knew anything at all about my old life, but I *did* want to have a place in New Orleans that I could come back to. Then I met Rob. She was having troubles of her own. She wanted to escape from her identity. I asked her how she'd like to trade identities. She said she'd like it swell. I told her to find a suitable apartment that would be something I could live in later on when I got ready to come back to New Orleans, and about what I was willing to pay for it."

"What name did you take?" I asked.

"Rob's."

"For how long?"

"For not more than two or three days."

"Then what?"

She said, "I suddenly realized what damning evidence I was manufacturing. If my husband's lawyers found out about it, they would show that I had gone away and started living under an assumed name. That would have been a confession of guilt, so I took my own name back. That simply meant there were two Edna Cutlers. One of them was Rob who was living in New Orleans, and the other was the real Edna Cutler."

I said, "Very, very interesting. It would make even the most hard-boiled judge cry into his law books."

"I'm not asking for sympathy. I'm only asking for justice."

I said, "All right, now let's cut out the comedy. *You* didn't think this up."

"What do you mean?"

"You didn't think up all that scheme for letting your husband hit the jackpot, and then find out the machine was empty."

"I don't get you."

I said, "I've known lots of lawyers. There have perhaps been four or five who could have thought up a trick like that, but the point is it took a lawyer to do it and it took a darned ingenious lawyer to do it."

"But I tell you it wasn't any scheme. I didn't think it up."

I said, "That brings us back to our friend, Paul G. Nostrander."

"What about him?"

"You knew him?"

She hesitated for several seconds over that question. I grinned while she was groping for an answer, then went on to say, "You never expected that question would be put to you in just that way, did you, Edna? You hadn't thought up your answer on that."

She said defiantly, "No. I didn't know him."

I saw Roberta Fenn's face show surprise.

I said, "That's where you're making your fatal mistake."

"What do you mean?"

I said, "Nostrander's secretary will probably remember that you were in the office. His books will show that, at least at the start, he received a fee from you. The people at Jack O'Leary's Bar will remember that you were in there together. They'll trap you in perjury. Your husband would spend a fortune on private detectives tracking all that stuff down. They'd bring that out in court, and a judge would realize you'd simply—"

She interrupted me to say, "All right, I knew him."

"How well?"

"I—I'd consulted him."

"And what did he tell you?"

"Told me that the only thing for me to do was to quit worrying, and," she went on triumphantly, as she realized the strength of this new defense, "he told me not to do anything at all until papers were served on me, that as soon as papers were served on me to let him know."

I said, "That's a swell line. Nostrander's dead. He can't contradict you on that, you know."

She contented herself with glaring at me, but made no other denial.

I turned to Roberta. "You knew him?"

"Yes."

"How did you meet him?"

Edna said quickly, "He is trying to get you to say that I introduced you to him. You met him in a bar, didn't you, Rob?"

Roberta didn't say anything.

I grinned. "That's another weak point in your story, Edna. I think you've already told Roberta too much."

"I haven't told her anything."

I said to Roberta, "Skip that. You don't have to lie, and if you're afraid of offending Edna, you can simply keep quiet and let it go at that. Now, why did you avoid Nostrander?"

"What do you mean?"

I said, "You stayed on in the apartment. You hung around the French Quarter for almost a year. You ate at the Bourbon House. You were seen quite frequently in Jack O'Leary's Bar. According to Edna's own story, you were supposed to get an apartment and stay there until she came back to live in New Orleans. Then, almost overnight, you moved out of the Quarter. You started living uptown. You studied stenography. You never went back to any of your old haunts. You carefully avoided meeting Nostrander. It wasn't until Edna gave Archibald Smith a letter to you that you went back to your old haunts in the French Quarter. You thought you were safe by that time. You weren't. Someone told Nostrander you'd been seen there. Nostrander started doing a little detective work. I don't know just how he went about it, but he may have done the same thing I did. In any event, he found you. He'd been looking for you for two years.

"Now why did you suddenly leave the French Quarter?"

Edna said, "You don't have to answer that question, Rob."

"You don't either one of you have to answer anything," I said, "not now. But when the police ask those questions, you're going to *have* to answer them."

"Why will the police ask them?" Edna asked.

"Don't you see?"

"No."

"Where were you about half-past two on Thursday morning?" I asked.

"To whom are you talking?" Edna demanded. "You're looking at me. You mean Roberta, don't you?"

"No. I mean *you*."

"What's that got to do with it?"

I said, "The police haven't put all the pieces of the jigsaw puzzle together yet, but when they do, this is the way the picture will look. You had a slick scheme to rob your husband of his triumph. Nostrander was mixed up in that scheme. So was Roberta Fenn. Roberta didn't know the details. Nostrander did. He's the one who thought the whole thing up.

"It was a swell scheme. It worked like a charm. Your husband should have been thrown into such a panic that he'd start paying through the nose. But your husband happens to be made of a little sterner stuff. He came on to New Orleans to investigate. He got in touch with the process server who served the papers. He'll probably get in touch with private detectives, if he hasn't a staff of them in New Orleans already. He'd have found out about Nostrander. Nostrander would have been the key witness. If Nostrander was put on the carpet on a charge of conspiracy, he might talk. If he talked, you'd lose a lot of money. If he didn't talk, you stood to make a big shakedown. There was one way of insuring Nostrander's silence. That was with a thirty-eight caliber bullet right in the middle of the heart. Better women than you have succumbed to less urgent temptations."

She said, "You're crazy."

I said, "That's the way the police are going to reason."

She glanced almost helplessly at Roberta Fenn.

"Now then," I said, "suppose you tell me just how you became acquainted with Archibald C. Smith, and why you happened to give him a letter to Roberta."

There seemed to be genuine surprise on her face. "Smith! Good heavens, what's that old fossil got to do with it?"

"That's what I want to know."

"Now I know you're crazy. He hasn't *anything* to do with it."

"Well, how did you happen to meet him? What's—"

The doorbell rang sharply.

"See who it is," I said to Edna.

She went to the telephone, pressed the button, said, "Who is it?"

Looking at her face, I knew from the expression of sheer terror what the answer was.

"Have you got any things here?" I asked Roberta. "A bag, clothes, anything?"

She shook her head. "I left the apartment without anything. I telegraphed Edna collect and she wired me money to come here. I haven't had a chance to buy anything. I—"

"Grab everything you've got," I said, "everything that would indicate you'd been here. Let's get going."

"I don't understand," she said.

I said to Edna, "Press the buzzer that opens the downstairs door. Take all these extra cigarette butts from the ash tray, and throw them out of the window. Be putting on that housecoat when they come to the door."

I saw Edna's hand groping for the button which controlled the buzzer.

"Who is it?" Roberta asked.

Edna turned to her. Her quivering lips couldn't answer.

"The police, of course," I said, grabbed Roberta's wrist, and rushed her to the door.

CHAPTER SIXTEEN

THERE WAS A BEND in the corridor about twenty feet from Edna's door. I kept my hand on Roberta's wrist, guiding her down the corridor and around this bend.

"But what—" she said. "Why—"

"Hush," I whispered. "Wait."

There were steps on the stairs.

"If it's one man," I whispered, "we wait here. If it's two men, we beat it."

There were two men. They came walking down the corridor, the heavy tread of beefy men. We could hear knuckles on Edna's door.

I peeked around the corner and saw two broad backs. I had a glimpse of Edna's white face; then the two men pushed their way into the room. I waited until the door closed, turned to Roberta, and beckoned.

She followed me down the hall.

At the head of the stairs she asked, "Why would we have waited if there had only been one?"

"They hunt in couples. If one had gone up, it would have meant the other was sitting in the car, waiting. With both of them in Edna's room, it should mean the coast is clear. At any rate, let's hope."

We went down the stairs. I pushed open the door and held it for Roberta. A police car was parked in front of the apartment. No one was in it.

"Let's go," I said.

We walked down the street.

"Not too fast."

"I feel as though something were chasing me. I want to run."

"Don't do it. Look up at me and laugh. Slow down. Here, let's stop and look in this window."

We paused, looked casually in a store window, then started walking again. Slowly I guided her around the corner.

"Know anyone else here?" I asked.

"No."

I said, "Okay, we go into a restaurant and eat. Had dinner?"

"No. We were just going out for dinner when you rang the bell. Edna was just out of the tub."

We strolled along the street. Once or twice she tried to ask me questions. I told her to wait. We found a good-looking restaurant with booths, went in, and selected a quiet booth off in the corner away from the door. The waiter brought a menu, and I ordered two daiquiri cocktails.

The waiter withdrew.

I said, "Keep your voice down low. Tell me how much you know about Edna's little scheme."

"Nothing," she said. "It happened just the way you doped it out, only I didn't know she was expecting any papers to be served on her."

"Why was Nostrander so anxious to see you?"

She said, "He fell for me. It was very annoying as far as I was concerned."

I said, "You don't mean that you moved out of the apartment, changed your whole style of living, simply because some man whom you didn't like was making passes at you."

"Well—well, not exactly."

"Why, then?"

"I'd rather let it go just the way it is."

I shook my head. "You can't."

She said, "Well, to tell you the truth, in part I got tired of the life I was living. I wasn't working. I was getting all of my expenses paid simply to stay there and take the name of Edna Cutler. I wasn't getting up until along about eleven or twelve o'clock in the morning. I'd go to breakfast, take a little walk, pick up some magazines, come back, read and doze during the afternoon, go out about seven o'clock for a bite to eat, come back, take a bath, put on my glad rags, take a lot of care with my make-up, and groom myself up to the minute. Then I'd either have a date, or else I'd drift across to one of the bars, and—well, you know how it is in New Orleans. It isn't like any other city on earth. A girl sits in the bar, and men pick her up. They don't think anything of it, and neither does the girl. In any other city, you'd wonder what sort she was, but—well, New Orleans is New Orleans."

The waiter brought our daiquiris. We touched glasses, took the first sip.

The waiter stood by the table, exerting a silent pressure for our orders.

"Could you bring some oysters on the half shell with a lot of cocktail sauce, some horseradish and lemon?" I asked. "Then bring us some of those cold, peppered shrimp, some onion soup, a steak about three inches thick, done medium rare, some French-fried onions, shoestring potatoes, cut some French bread, put on lots of butter, sprinkle on just a trace of garlic, put it in the oven, let it get good and hot so the butter melts all through the bread, put some sparkling Burgundy on the ice, and after that bring us a dish of ice cream, a huge pot of coffee, and the check."

The waiter never batted an eyelash. "I could do that very nicely, sir."

"How about you?" I asked Roberta.

"I could go for that in a big way."

I nodded to the waiter, waited until the green curtains had dropped back into place, and said suddenly to Roberta, "Where were you at two-thirty a.m. Thursday?"

She said, "If I told you what happened that night, you wouldn't believe it."

"Bad as that?"

"Yes."

"Tell me then."

She said, "I'd kept away from Nostrander. He didn't know I was in New Orleans; then he found me. You were there when he found me. You heard what he said. It was the first time I'd seen him for two years. I didn't want to have a scene in front of you. The last time I had seen him, he had been absolutely crazy about me. In fact, he had a jealousy complex. That was one of the things which made him so distasteful to me. Whenever I'd try to go out with anyone else, he'd go absolutely crazy—I mean that literally. He was a very brilliant man, but completely unstable. Heaven help the woman who ever married him! He wouldn't have let even the milkman come to the house."

"Is that why you took him out in the corridor the night I was at your apartment?"

"Yes. I knew he had a gun, and I was afraid he was going to do something desperate. When he saw you there he almost pulled his gun. I took him out in the corridor. He was insanely jealous of you. I told him I'd never seen you before, that you were a business visitor. He wouldn't believe me. He thought, finding you in my apartment, that you were the privileged boy friend. He pulled his gun, said he'd shoot me and kill himself if I didn't go out with him, and went through the old dramatics. So I told him that the reason I hadn't seen him, and the reason I hadn't gone out with him, was because of that very trait in his character, that if he'd put that gun back in his pocket and quit all that crazy jealousy, I'd go out to dinner with him, and we'd have a few drinks."

"He wanted to know all about me?" I asked.

"Oh, of course."

"What did you tell him?"

"I told him the truth. I told him you were a detective who was trying to find out something about a man by the name of Smith in order to close up an estate."

"Did he ask you who Smith was?"

"Oh, certainly. You mention any man's name, and he'd pounce on it like a hawk swooping on a baby chick. He'd want to know all about him, who he was, where he came from, how long you'd known him, and all that. I told him Smith was a friend of Edna's."

"And he did all that out in the corridor?"

"No, not out in the corridor. I told him that I didn't have time to stand there and argue with him. I was going to have to get rid of you if I was going to dinner with him. So he agreed to wait."

"That's the point I'm interested in," I said. "Where did he wait?"

"He said he'd wait outside somewhere, and come back after you'd gone."

"Did he?"

"What?"

"Come back after I'd left?"

"Yes. Within less than a minute."

She saw the expression on my face. "What's the matter? What are you scowling about?"

"I was trying to think back," I said. "As I remember it, there's only one string of apartments in that building. It's over a storeroom, and the corridor runs the length of the building, with apartments on both sides, isn't that right?"

"Yes."

"There are no bends or crooks in the corridor where a man might hide?"

"No."

"I didn't see him there when I went out."

"He might have gone over to the far end and flattened himself in the shadows where he could watch you, without your knowing he was there. That's the way he would do things. He was secretive and liked to spy on people. Good heavens, when I was living there in the Quarter, you'd have thought I was an enemy alien, and he was the whole F.B.I. He snooped around, watched my apartment window with binoculars. When I'd go out with anyone, he'd be hanging around somewhere to find out what time I got in. I didn't even dare to take a boy friend upstairs to have a drink—"

The waiter appeared with a tray, put dishes on the table. We started eating.

"Want to hear the rest of it?" she asked, after a few moments.

"After dinner," I said. "Let's concentrate on eating now. I'm hungry."

We ate our way through dinner. I could see that her nerves were relaxing. The wine and the food generated a mood of expansive friendship.

"Know something, Donald?"

"What?"

"I feel that I can trust you. I'm going to tell you the whole truth."

"Why not?"

She pushed away her plate, accepted one of my cigarettes, and leaned forward for a light. She reached up with her hands and held my hand and the match in both of hers. Her hands were soft and warm, the skin smooth. "Paul and I went out to dinner. He was going to kill you," she said.

"He got drunk and crazy jealous again. He began asking me a lot of questions about you. He wouldn't believe you were a detective. Finally I got sore, and told him that he hadn't changed a bit in the last two years, that I'd tried to let him down easy once by simply moving out, but this time I was giving it to him the hard way; that I didn't want to see him again ever, and I didn't want to have anything to do with him; that if he ever tried to force himself on me, I'd call the officers."

"What did he do then?"

"He did something that frightened me, and at the same time it made me laugh."

"What?"

"He grabbed my purse."

"Why? So you wouldn't have any money?"

"That's what I thought at the time, but I realized later what it was."

"You mean he wanted your key?"

"Yes."

"Where were you when he took your purse?"

"In Jack O'Leary's Bar down in the Quarter. That was always his regular hangout."

"And just what did he do?"

She said, "I was telling him that I was tired of the way he did things, that I couldn't stand that insane jealousy, and that I wasn't ever going to see him again.

"The bar was crowded. I didn't know what he'd do, but I did feel that if he tried to pull a gun or make any threats, there were enough people around to grab him before he could do anything. Even if there weren't, I was just tired of living in perpetual terror of that man. Until he fell in love with me, he was simply wonderful."

"You met him through Edna?"

"Yes."

"How did he feel toward Edna?"

"I think he was—well, perhaps, playing around. I think he picked her up there in Jack O'Leary's Bar, and they were going together for a while; then Edna told him her troubles, and he worked out this scheme by which she could fleece her husband. That must have been it. I can look back now and put two and two together."

"But Edna never told you that?"

"No. She never confided in me the real reason she wanted me to take the apartment in her name. Just gave me some excuses as she did you when you first asked her.

She didn't let me know where she was. Paul Nostrander was the only one who knew that, but he claimed *he* didn't. Every month Paul would give me enough money to cover all my living expenses, the apartment, clothes, meals, beauty treatments, and all the rest."

"Did you give him the papers when you were served?"

"No. I tried to, but he wouldn't take them. He said he had no authority. He told me Edna had simply arranged with him to give me money from a fund she'd left with him. He claimed *he* didn't actually know where she was, and had no means of reaching her. He said she'd given him fifteen hundred dollars to apply on my expenses, that the money had nearly all been spent."

"All right, you told Nostrander where to get off, and he took your purse. Then what?"

"Without a word, he walked out."

"Pay the check?"

"They don't have any checks there at Jack O'Leary's. You pay for the drinks as you get them."

"So he walked out and left you sitting there?"

"Yes."

"What did you do?"

"I sat around there for a while, and a couple of soldiers who were on the loose started making eyes at me, and I thought, after all, why not? The boys were going to be shipped somewhere pretty soon. They were entitled to as much of a good time as I could show them, so I smiled back at them. They came over, and we had quite an evening. They were awfully nice boys, but they knew nothing whatever about New Orleans. It was their first night in town. They came from Milwaukee. I took them around and showed them some of the sights, told them stories about the Quarter, drank with them until they were just about able to navigate, and left them."

"What did you do?"

"I walked home, every single, blessed step of the way."

"You didn't take a cab?"

"No. I didn't have my purse; I didn't have a cent."

"And how did you intend to get in if you didn't have a key?"

"I had a key."

"I thought you said he took your key."

"Took one of them, but there's another key in the bottom of my mailbox. I always leave it there, just in case of an emergency. You see, there's a spring lock on the door, and sometimes when I run down to the corner to get things from the grocery store, I'll forget to take my key along, so I always leave an extra one there in the mailbox."

"What time did you leave the soldiers?"

"Oh, about two o'clock, I guess. Somewhere around there."

"And you walked home?"

"Yes."

"What time did you get there?"

"At exactly twenty minutes past two."

I said, "Why are you so positive in your time? Did you hear a shot?"

"No."

"What did you hear?"

"I didn't hear. I saw."

"What?"

"My friend, Archibald C. Smith."

I did a little thinking over that one, and said, "Wait a minute. You *couldn't* have seen him. He was in New York that night."

She smiled. "I saw him plainly."

"What did he say to you? What did you talk about?"

"I didn't talk with him. I saw him, but he didn't see me."

"Where?"

"Down in front of my apartment."

"When?"

"Just as I'm telling you, at twenty minutes past two."

"Go ahead," I said. "What happened?"

She said, "I was very close to the apartment when he came past in a taxicab. He got out of the cab and ran up the three steps to the street door and rang the bell of my apartment."

"Are you certain it was your apartment?"

"Well, reasonably certain. I could see the position of his finger. I couldn't see the exact button he was touching, but it was—yes, it must have been my bell he was ringing."

"And what happened after he found you weren't home?"

"I don't know."

"Why? Didn't he turn back and see you coming along the sidewalk just a step or two behind him?"

"No."

"What did he do?"

"He went in."

"You mean he entered the apartment house?"

"Yes."

"How did he get in?"

"Somebody in my apartment pushed the buzzer for him."

"And what did you do?"

"Up to that time I'd thought Paul Nostrander had taken my purse so that I wouldn't have any money, and so he could go through it and—well, see if there was anything in there, a diary, or perhaps a letter from you, or something of that sort."

I nodded, keeping my eyes on her. "And after you heard the buzzer sound?"

"Then I knew why he'd really taken it. He'd gone up to my apartment, let himself in with my key, and was waiting up there."

"A delicate approach," I said.

"It wasn't entirely that," she said. "Of course that was part of it. The other part was that he'd been accusing me all evening of being intimate with someone. You see, the way I'd disappeared had made him feel that way. He'd advertised for me in the paper. A personal ad that had run for almost two years."

"I know. I saw it."

"Well, naturally, he thought I'd gone away with some man. I knew it was only a question of time until I'd run into him on the street somewhere, but I felt that the longer it was put off the more chance he'd have to fall in love with someone else and forget me. But he has that peculiar complex some men have—he only wants someone he can't get. You know how some men are?"

I nodded.

"There he was," she went on bitterly, "in my apartment, with his gun, and probably about two-thirds drunk, sitting there on the bed, waiting for me, and determined that he was going to find out whether anyone was sufficiently intimate with me to come to my apartment. He'd insisted that I'd promised you that if you'd go out without making any trouble, you could come back later, and—well, you know."

"And so," I said, "Archibald C. Smith pressed the doorbell at twenty minutes past two—and walked right into the middle of that situation."

"Yes—he must have gone on up."

"And you think Archibald Smith thought you would be in your apartment at that hour of the night, and would answer the bell?"

"Well, he certainly must have thought I'd be there, and the bell would get me up. It was reasonable to suppose that I'd at least pick up the telephone and ask who was there."

"Did *you* hear any shot?" I asked.

"No."

"Would you if one had been fired?"

"I don't think so, not the way it was muffled by the pillow."

"What did you do?"

"I crossed the street. I tried to look up to the window of my apartment. I couldn't see anything. The shade was drawn."

"Then what?"

"I started walking back toward town."

"At what time?"

"It must have been just before two-thirty. When I had reached the corner, Marilyn Winton drove by. She was in a car with two other people—a man and a woman."

"You know her?"

"Oh, I know who she is, and we speak when we meet in the hall. Her apartment is almost directly across from mine."

"Then what did you do?"

"Went to one of the little hotels in the Quarter which isn't too particular. I used an assumed name, because I thought Paul might try calling all the hotels."

"And then what?"

"Shortly before nine I walked all the way down to the apartment. I wanted to get my purse, some of my toilet articles, grab a taxi, and go to work. There were a bunch of cars around the place, and a man who was standing at the curb told me a murder had been committed, said some lawyer had been found dead in a woman's apartment, and the woman was missing. The police were looking for her."

"And what did you do then?"

"Like a ninny, instead of making a clean breast of the situation and explaining it while it could have been explained, I got in a panic and dashed back to the hotel. I sent Edna a wire telling her to send money quickly, waiving identification and making the draft payable to that assumed name I'd registered under."

"You wired?"

"Yes."

"Didn't you try telephoning collect?"

"Yes."

"Got her?"

"No. She didn't answer."

"She answered the wire?"

"That afternoon. I got the hotel to cash it and took a late train to Shreveport."

The waiter came and cleared away the dishes, brought the ice cream and coffee.

"Can you trust Edna?" I asked.

"I used to think I could. Now I'm not so certain. She acted strangely."

I said, "It helps Edna's case a lot having Nostrander out of the way."

"Yes. I can see that—now."

"It might make a motive for murder."

"You mean that she might have killed him?"

"The police might think so."

"But she was in Shreveport."

"Not when you telephoned."

"Well—no, perhaps not."

"It was late the next afternoon before she sent you the money?"

"Yes."

We finished our ice cream, sat smoking cigarettes and sipping coffee. Neither of us said much. We were both thinking.

"What do I do next?" she asked.

"Got any money?"

"Some left from what Edna sent me. Tell me, Donald, what *should* I do? Should I go back to the police and tell my story?"

"Not yet, and not now."

"Why?"

"It's too late now. You've missed the boat."

"Couldn't I explain the—"

"Not now, you couldn't."

"Why?"

I said, "You didn't murder him, did you?"

She looked as though I'd thrown something at her.

I said, "All right, someone did. That someone wouldn't like anything better than to have the police blame things on you."

"Well, can't I do myself more good by being there to block that very thing?"

"I don't think so."

"Why?"

"If you're out of circulation for a while the real murderer will then try to make you the goat by planting evidence, making false statements, and things of that sort. Then you'll have the chance to find out who this is. Reel out lots of rope and see if we can't hang somebody."

"Not me, I hope."

I met her eyes, raised my coffee cup.

"I hope."

I paid the check, inquired if there was a telephone booth in the restaurant, found there was, closeted myself in it, and called the airport at New Orleans.

"This is Detective Lam at Shreveport talking," I said, and then so they wouldn't start asking questions as to whether I was on the force at Shreveport or a private detective, I started talking fast. "On Wednesday noon you had a passenger for New York. That passenger turned right around at New York and came back to New Orleans. The name was Emory G. Hale."

The voice at the other end of the line said, "Just a minute and I'll consult the records."

I waited for a minute or so during which I could hear papers rustling; then the voice said, "That's right. Emory G. Hale. New York and back."

"You wouldn't know what he looked like? I wouldn't be able to get a description?"

"No. I don't remember him. Just a minute."

I heard him say, "Anyone remember selling a ticket

to a man named Hale for New York on Wednesday?
Shreveport police calling. . . . No, I'm sorry we don't
have anyone who remembers him."

"When you book a passenger, don't you take his
weight?"

"Yes."

I said, "What did Hale weigh?"

"Just a minute. I have that right here. He weighed—
let's see—yes, here we are. He weighed a hundred and
forty-six."

I thanked him and hung up.

Emory G. Hale would have tipped the beam at something over two hundred pounds.

I came out of the telephone booth.

"What is it?" Roberta asked. "Bad news?"

"Want to go to California?" I asked.

"Yes."

I said, "I think we can hire a car to take us to Fort
Worth and a plane from Fort Worth will get us into
Los Angeles tomorrow morning."

"Why California?"

"Because this state is very, very hot so far as you're
concerned."

"Won't we attract attention?"

"Yes. The more the better."

"What do you mean?"

I said, "People speculate about a couple whom they
don't know. The thing to do is make them know us.
We get acquainted with everybody from the driver of
the rented automobile to the passengers on the plane.
We're husband and wife. We left Los Angeles to come
east on our honeymoon. We've just got a wire that your
mother had a spell with her heart, and we're rushing
back to be with her. It's an interrupted honeymoon.
People will sympathize with us, remember us in that
capacity. If the police teletype starts clicking out a description of you as being wanted for murder, no one

will ever connect that description with the poor little bride who is so worried about her mother."

"When do we start?" she asked.

I said, "As soon as I telephone for an automobile," and went back into the telephone booth.

CHAPTER SEVENTEEN

AT DAYLIGHT Sunday morning we were skimming over Arizona. Gradually the desert had ceased to be a vague, gray sea beneath us and had acquired form, substance, and color. The higher buttes thrust their rim rocks up at the plane, catching the first vague suggestion of light. Down below, the deeper canyons and dry washes were filled with shadows. The stars pinpointed themselves into a bluish green oblivion. As we sped westward, the roar of the twin motors echoed from the jagged rim rocks around the buttes below. The east assumed a rosy glow. The tops of the buttes were bathed in champagne. We sped over the desert as though trying to flee from the sun. Then abruptly the sun shot over the horizon, and the bright rays pounced upon us. The fainter colors of dawn gave place to dazzling bits of brilliance where sun splashed against the eastern edges of the cliffs, accentuating the dark shadows. The sun climbed higher. We could see the shadow of the plane scudding along below us. Then we were over the Colorado River, and into California. The roar of the motors faded to the peculiar whining sound which precedes a landing, and we were down in a little desert stopping place where the airport lunch counter gave us steaming hot coffee and bacon and eggs while the plane was refueling.

Once more we were off. Great snow-capped mountains appeared ahead, guarding the edge of the desert like gray-haired sentinels. The plane jumped and twisted like something alive in the narrow confines of a pass between two big mountains, and then, so abruptly that it seemed there was no appreciable period of transition, the desert fell behind, and we were skimming over a citrus country in which orange and lemon groves, laid out in checkerboard squares, marched by in an endless procession. The red roofs of white stucco houses showed in startling contrast to the vivid green of the citrus trees. Dozens of cities, constantly growing larger and crowding closer together as we neared Los Angeles, spoke of the prosperity of the country below.

Then they shrouded the plane. I looked across at Roberta. "Won't be long now," I told her.

She smiled somewhat wistfully. "I think it's the best honeymoon trip I ever had," she said.

Then, almost without warning, the plane was swooping down out of the sky, gliding toward a long cement runway. The wheels dipped smoothly to the earth, and we were in Los Angeles.

I said, "Okay. Here we are. We go to a hotel, and I'll get in touch with my partner."

"The Bertha Cool you've been talking about?"

"Yes."

"Do you think she'll like me?"

"No."

"Why?"

"She doesn't like good-looking young women—particularly when she thinks I do."

"Why? Afraid she's going to lose you?"

"Just on principle," I said. "She probably doesn't have any reason."

"Do we—that is, register under our own names?"

"No."

"But, Donald, you—I mean I—"

"You register as Roberta Lam," I said. "I register

under my own name. From now on we're brother and sister. Our mother is very low. We hurried to be at her side."

"And I'm Roberta Lam?"

"Yes."

"Donald, aren't you putting yourself in a dangerous position?"

"Why?"

"Giving me the protection of your name, when you know I'm wanted by the police."

"I didn't know you were wanted by the police. Why didn't you tell me?"

She smiled. "It's a nice alibi, Donald, but it won't work. They'll ask you why it was you spirited me around, using an assumed name and an assumed relationship if you didn't realize that police were looking for me under my own name."

"The answer to that is very simple," I said. "You're a material witness. I think I can use you to solve a murder. I'm keeping you with me. In place of reporting to Bertha Cool by letter, I'm taking you with me so she can hear your entire story."

She was silent for several seconds, then said, "I feel quite certain Bertha Cool is going to hate me from the minute she sees me."

"She probably won't shower any too much cordiality on you."

We went to a hotel, registered. The clerk listened to my story about our dying mother, as I told him that I must hurry to a telephone. He pointed out the phone booth to me.

I called Bertha's unlisted number. She didn't answer.

I went up to my room, called Bertha once more. This time a colored maid answered.

"Mrs. Cool?" I asked.

"She ain't here now."

"When will she be in?"

"I can't tell."

"Where did she go?"

"Fishing."

"When she comes in, tell her to call—no, tell her that Mr. Donald Lam called, and that he'll call every hour until he gets her."

"Yes sir. I think the fishin' was early this morning. I think the tide was goin' to be just right at seven-thirty. I rather 'spect her back pretty soon."

"I'll call every hour. Tell her that I said that. Be sure she gets that message—that I'll call every hour."

I climbed into the luxury of a hot bath, lay soaking for ten or fifteen minutes, then got up and turned on the cold shower. I rubbed myself into a glow, dressed, shaved, and stretched out for forty winks.

I was awakened by Roberta gently opening and closing the door of the connecting room.

"What is it?" I asked.

"Time for you to call Mrs. Cool again."

I groaned, picked up the telephone, gave the number to the operator, and waited.

This time Bertha was home—evidently, by the sound of things, just coming into the apartment as the telephone rang. I heard the maid call her, and could hear her hurried steps thudding across the floor, then the sound of her voice rasping at me through the receiver. "For God's sake, why don't you stay put? What do you think this agency's made of? Money? When you want a conference, why don't you use the telephone? I've tried to educate you to that a dozen different times."

"All through?" I asked.

"Hell, no!" she said belligerently. "I haven't even started."

"All right, I'll call you back when you're through. One doesn't argue with a lady."

I dropped the phone gently back on the hook, abruptly cutting off Bertha's rage-shrilled voice.

Roberta's eyes were big. I could see she was frightened.

"Donald, are you going to fight over me?"

"Probably."

"Please don't."

"We have to fight over something."

"What do you mean?"

"Bertha. You have to massage her with a club in order to keep *her* from beating *your* brains out. She doesn't mean anything by it. It's just the way she's made. She can't help it. When you see she's getting her fist cocked, you beat her to the punch. That's all. I'm going to sleep again. Don't bother to waken me. You go ahead and get some sleep."

"Aren't you going to call her again?"

"After a while."

Roberta smiled somewhat wistfully and said, "You're a funny boy."

"Why?" I asked, settling myself back on the bed.

"Nothing," she said, and walked back to her room.

It took me ten or fifteen minutes to get back to sleep. I must have slept for a couple of hours. When I wakened, I rang Bertha Cool again.

"Hello, Bertha. This is Donald."

"You damn little whippersnapper! You dirty little upstart! What the hell do you mean by pulling a stunt like that. I'll teach you to hang up on me! Why, dammit, I'll—"

"I'll call you back in a couple of hours," I said, and hung up.

Roberta came in in about an hour. "I didn't hear you get up."

"You were sleeping. Guess you're pretty tired."

"I was."

She sat on the arm of my chair, her hand on my shoulder, looking down at the paper.

"Did you call Mrs. Cool again?"

"Yes."

"What did she say?"

"Same thing."

"What did you do, Donald?"

"Same thing."

"I thought you were anxious to talk with her."

"I am."

She laughed. "You've taken planes and dashed across the country in order to have this conference, and now you're sitting around doing nothing."

"That's right."

"I don't understand it."

"I'm waiting for Bertha to cool off."

"Do you think she will? Don't you think she'll get more angry than ever?"

"She's so mad right now she could eat a dish of ten-penny nails without cream or sugar. She's also curious. Curiosity persists until it's satisfied. Rage dies down after a while. That's the secret of dealing with Bertha. Want the funny paper?"

Her laugh was low and nervous. "Not now," she said. "What's this?"

She bent forward to read a paragraph in the paper I was holding. I could feel her hair brush against mine.

I held the paper steady until she had finished; then I dropped it to the floor, turned my body sideways. She slid down into my lap.

I kissed her.

For a moment her lips were against mine, a warm oval hungry for a caress; then suddenly her hazel eyes were looking steadily at me. She was holding her head back and smiling a little. "I wondered when that was coming," she said.

"What?"

"The pass."

I eased her gently to the floor. "It wasn't a pass. It was a kiss."

"Oh."

She sat there for a moment, looking up at me, and then laughed again. "You *are* funny."

"Why?"

"Oh, I don't know. Just lots of things. Do you like me, Donald?"

"Yes."

"Do you think I—committed a murder?"

"I don't know."

"You think I may have?"

"Yes."

"Is that what's holding you back?"

"Is something holding me back?"

"Donald, I wish you wouldn't do this for me."

She was sitting at my feet now, her fingers interlaced across my knee. "I think you're a *very* wonderful person."

"I'm not."

"And you've certainly been wonderful to me. I don't know whether I can ever tell you what it's meant to me to have someone act—well, decent. You've given me back a lot of faith in human nature. The reason I disappeared that first time was—oh, it was mixed up in something sordid and brutal and frightful. I can't even tell you about it. I don't want you to know what it was, but it ruined my faith in human nature. I came to the conclusion that people, particularly men, were—" The doorknob rattled into a quick turn. Someone lunged against the door.

Roberta looked at me in startled surprise. "Police?" she whispered.

I motioned toward the connecting room.

She took two steps toward the door of her room, then glided back. I felt her hand on my cheek, under my chin, lifting my head. Before I realized what she was doing, her lips were clinging to mine.

Knuckles banged angrily on the door.

Roberta whispered, "If this should be it—that's thanks, and good-by."

She moved across the room like the shadow of a bird floating across a meadow. The door gently closed.

Knuckles banging again at my door, and then Bertha

Cool's angry voice, "Donald, open that door!"

I crossed the room and opened the door. "What the hell do you think you're trying to do?"

"Sit down, Bertha. Take this chair. You've seen the papers, I take it? You must have done a nice job tracing my call to this hotel. Probably cost you a good tip."

Bertha said, "You're a hell of a partner, disappearing like that without letting anyone know where you are! Hale has telephoned from New Orleans. He's sore. He says he thinks you've given him a double-cross, says he isn't going to pay any bonus or anything else. He's going to hold us responsible for breach of contract."

"Have a cigarette, Bertha?"

She took a deep breath, started to say something, then changed her mind; and her lips clamped together in a hard, thin line.

I lit a cigarette.

Bertha said, "That's the trouble with making you a partner, you little runt. I pick you up off the streets when you are so hungry your belt buckle is carving its initials in your backbone. I stake you to a meal and give you a job, and within a couple of years you've muscled your way into the partnership. Now you're running the business with a high hand. I suppose next thing I know, *I'll* be working for *you*."

I said, "You may as well sit down. It sounds as though you're going to be here for a while."

She made no move to sit down. I walked over, stretched myself out on the bed once more, moved up an ash tray. Apparently Bertha had no slightest idea that Roberta Fenn was in the next room.

"You're damn right I'm going to be here for a while," Bertha said. "I'm going to stay right with you from now on—until we get this thing cleaned up. If I have to, I'll handcuff you to me. Now you put through a call to Mr. Hale in New Orleans and tell him where you are, tell him you came on here for a conference, that you didn't have time to notify him because it was too important, that you just got in. Try and square yourself and the agency the best way you can."

I continued to smoke without making any move toward the telephone.

"Did you hear me?"

"Yes."

"Are you going to do it?"

"No."

Bertha walked over to the telephone, jerked the receiver up, said to the operator, "Mr. Lam wants to talk with Emory G. Hale in New Orleans. You'll find him at the Monteleone Hotel. It's a person-to-person call. He'll talk with no one else. . . . What's that? . . . Yes, I'm—yes, I know. It's Mr. Lam's room. *He* wants to talk. . . . Yes, of course he's here."

She held the phone so tight I could see the skin stretched white across her knuckles. She said, "Very well," and turned to me.

I said, "What is it?"

"They want you to okay the call."

I made no move toward the telephone.

She shoved the instrument at me. "Okay that call!"

I continued to smoke.

"You mean you aren't going to?"

"That's right."

She slammed the receiver back into its cradle so hard that I looked for the instrument to fly to pieces. "Of all the damned exasperating bastards! Of all the ill-mannered, impudent—" Her voice rose almost to a scream, then choked in her throat.

"May as well sit down, Bertha."

She stood looking down at me for a moment, then said abruptly, "Now listen, lover, don't be like that, Bertha gets excited, but it's because she's been worried about you. Bertha thought something had happened and someone had put a bullet in you."

"I'm sorry."

"Sorry! You never even bothered to send me a wire.

153

You—now listen, lover, Bertha doesn't like to get like this. You've got me terribly nervous."

"Sit down and you'll get over being so nervous."

She walked over to the chair and sat down.

"Help yourself to a cigarette," I said. "It will steady your nerves."

"Why did you leave New Orleans?" she asked after a minute or two.

"I thought we should have a conference."

"What about?"

"I'll tell you when you've quieted down."

"Tell me now, Donald."

"No, not now."

"Why?"

"You're too excited."

"I'm not excited."

"Wait until I can see that you're really enjoying your cigarette, and then we'll talk."

She settled back in the chair and went through the motions of relaxing. But her eyes were still hard and angry.

I waited until she had puffed her way to the end of the cigarette.

"Going to tell me now?"

"Have another cigarette."

She sat there, glowering at me. "I suppose it all gets back to the fact that money doesn't mean a damn thing to you. You've never had the responsibilities of running a business. Just because we've been lucky with the first few partnership cases doesn't mean that—"

"Haven't we been all over that before?" I interrupted.

She started to get up out of the chair, then, halfway up, dropped back again.

She didn't say anything, and neither did I. We sat there in silence for nearly fifteen minutes. Finally Bertha took another cigarette. She started it off with a deep drag.

"All right, lover," she said, "let's talk."

"What did you find out about that old murder case?" I asked.

"Donald, *why* did you want to know about that?"

I said, "I think it has something to do with what happened in New Orleans."

"Well, I haven't been able to get anything on it yet. I've got some people working on it. I should know by tomorrow afternoon."

"How about newspaper clippings?"

"I told Elsie Brand to go down to the library and copy stuff from the files of the newspapers. Donald, you've simply *got* to get busy and find that girl."

"Which one?"

"Roberta Fenn."

"I found her once."

"Well, find her twice," Bertha said with a flash of temper.

"I'm worried about Hale."

"What about him?"

"He's carrying water on both shoulders."

"Now you listen to me, Donald Lam. We aren't conducting a society to purify the motives of our clients. We're running a detective agency. We're trying to make money out of it. If a client comes to me and says he wants to find someone, and puts up the money, it's the money that really does the talking."

"So I gathered."

"And that's business."

"Perhaps."

"Oh, I know it isn't *your* way. You go around charging windmills. You think that just because we're running a detective agency, we're supposed to be knights of the Round Table. You find damsels in distress and fall for them, and they fall for you, and—"

"But I'm still worried about Hale."

"So am I. I'm afraid he's not going to pay us our bonus."

"Didn't you put the agreement in writing?"

"Well—well, there's a chance he might squirm out of it on a technicality—just a technicality, you understand. What worries you about him?"

I said, "Let's look at it this way. Hale came from New York. He hired us in Los Angeles to find a girl in New Orleans. It was absurdly easy to find her."

"But Hale didn't know that," she said.

"The hell he didn't. Hale knew exactly where she was living. He could have put his finger on her at any moment. He'd been out with her just before he came to see us."

"That may not mean anything."

I said, "All right, we'll pass that and go on to something else."

She said, "Nix on that stuff, Donald. That's what Hale said he wouldn't stand for."

"Why did he say that?"

"I don't know. Probably because he didn't want to be bothered by having us waste our time and his money on a lot of foolishness."

I said, "We found Roberta. You were to go and see her the next morning. Hale was supposed to be in New York. He wasn't in New York. He was in New Orleans."

"How do you know that?"

"Because I checked up at the airport. The man who traveled to New York and back using the name of Emory G. Hale weighed a hundred and forty-six pounds."

"Perhaps the weight was wrong."

I smiled at her.

"Oh, don't be so damned superior! Go ahead, if you feel that way about it. Tell me the rest of it."

I said, "You put in a call for Hale at New York. You couldn't get him, but Hale called you and *said* he was calling from New York, or some intermediate point where the plane was grounded. You don't know whether he was or not. No one knows. He could have been within a block of the hotel. All he needed was some girl to say into the telephone, 'New York is calling Mrs. Bertha Cool. Is this she? Hold the line, please.' "

Bertha's eyes were ominous. "Go ahead. Get it all out of your system."

"When he showed up in New Orleans the next morning and I told him I'd found Roberta Fenn and we started down to her apartment, he knew she wasn't there."

"How do you know that?"

"Because he went along with me."

"What does that have to do with it?"

"Don't you understand? She knew him as Archibald C. Smith. The minute she saw him, she would have said, 'Why, how do you do, Mr. Smith? What brings you here?' Then the cat would have been out of the bag. He knew that. Therefore, *if* he had thought she was there, he'd have sent me down alone to call on her."

Bertha was interested now. "Anything else?"

"Lots of it."

"What?"

"The only real witness to that exact time of the shooting is a girl by the name of Marilyn Winton. She's a nightclub hostess. She was just entering the apartment house when she heard the sound of the shot. She looked at her wrist watch a few minutes later. She places the shot as being at exactly two-thirty-two."

"What about her?"

I said, "Emory Hale was seen entering that apartment house at about twenty minutes past two."

"You mean that's where he was when he was supposed to have been in New York?"

"Yes."

"Who saw him?"

"I can't tell you."

Her face darkened. "What the hell do you mean you can't tell me?"

"Exactly that. It's confidential as yet."

She glared at me as though she wanted to bite my head off. "Some girl," she said. "Some little trollop who's trying to take you for a ride tells you that she saw Hale entering the apartment house, and you mustn't say anything, just keep it confidential. So you turn your own partner down because some little petticoat with a sweet smile looks languishingly up into your eyes, and gives you the works. Bosh!"

I said, "One other person told me that was true."

"Who?"

"Hale."

"Donald—do you mean to say that you talked with *him* about it? Why, the one thing that he impressed upon us was that, under no circumstances, were we to start speculating about him. He wanted—"

"Take it easy," I interrupted. "He didn't tell me about it in words. He told me about it by his actions."

"What do you mean?"

I said, "He became anxious to meet this Marilyn Winton. I arranged to take him to the nightclub. We poured four or five drinks down each other. He was trying to find out how much I knew. I was trying to find out what he wanted."

"Did you make him pay for the drinks?"

"Certainly. I may be dumb on financial matters, but I'm not that dumb."

"What did you find out?"

"He got to talking with Marilyn Winton about the time she'd heard the shot, whether she was absolutely certain it was two-thirty-two and not three o'clock."

"Well?"

"She told him that it was two-thirty-two by her wrist watch. So Hale admired the watch and asked her to let him look at it."

"Well, what's with that?"

"At the time," I said, "he was drinking Coca-Cola and gin."

"And what does that have to do with what we're talking about?" she demanded impatiently.

I said, "He put the drink down below the table, holding it in between his knees while he turned the wrist watch around, looking at it. A floor show was on, and the lights were dim. His right hand, holding the wrist watch, dropped below the table for a few seconds. After that he blew his nose a couple of times and whipped his handkerchief around rather promiscuously. Then he put the glass back on the table, and while he was doing that, put the wrist watch in the handkerchief. Then he handed the wrist watch back. Marilyn held a napkin to it. Then she moistened the napkin in a glass of water and moved it along her wrist just underneath the wrist watch."

"Don't bother me with all that stuff," Bertha said. "What's all that got to do with it? What do I care how many times he blew his nose? Just so he pays the money, he can blow his damn head off, for all I care. He—"

"You don't get it," I said. "The thing the girl did—putting water on her napkin and rubbing it along her wrist—that's the significant thing."

"Why?"

I said, "The wrist watch was sticky."

"I don't get you."

I said, "You dip a wrist watch in a glass of gin and Coca-Cola, leave it in there for a minute or so, and then bring it out, wipe it off hastily with a handkerchief, and the watch is apt to be sticky—enough sugar in the Coca-Cola, you know."

"And why the devil should anyone dip a wrist watch in a drink of gin and Coca-Cola?" Bertha asked.

"So that when the person who was wearing it was cross-examined about the *exact* time she heard the shot, she'd have to confess that a few days afterward she noticed her wrist watch was out of order, and she had to take it to a jeweler."

Bertha sat blinking at me as though I'd flashed a very bright light full in her eyes.

"I'll be damned!"

I didn't say anything, but just sat there, letting her think it over.

After a while she said, "Are you sure about the watch, Donald, that he dunked it in the drink?"

"No. I'm simply giving you the evidence. It's circumstantial."

"Why on earth would he have gone up to Roberta Fenn's apartment?"

"Two reasons."

"Roberta Fenn is one?"

"Yes. And the other's the dead lawyer, Nostrander."

"Why would Nostranger figure in it?"

I said, "Roberta Fenn was feeling pretty low. She went to New Orleans. Edna Cutler was in New Orleans. She's the wife of Marco Cutler. Marco was about to give her a terrific smear in a divorce action. Edna couldn't face the music. She went to New Orleans, got Roberta to pose as her double. When the papers arrived to be served on Edna, the process server served them on Roberta.

"Marco Cutler got his divorce. He didn't wait for the final decree. He married a wealthy woman who has ideas about such things. She may be going to have a baby. Edna Cutler chose that time to appear on the scene and calmly observe that *she'd* never heard of any divorce. It was a slick stunt. She's got him over a barrel unless he can prove fraud or collusion."

"Can he do that?"

"He might be trying."

"How?"

"By hiring detectives."

"What detectives?"

"Us."

Bertha's eyes kept blinking rapidly. "Fry me for an

oyster," she said at length, almost under her breath.

"Get it?" I asked.

"Of course I get it. Marco Cutler is in the millionaire class. If he'd hired us and told us what he wanted us to find out, we'd have soaked him good and proper. Moreover, we'd have been able to blackmail him. He got this New York lawyer to come out here, and because the man was from New York, we kept thinking it was a New York client that was involved in the case."

"Go ahead, you're doing fine."

"Then this lawyer, posing as a man by the name of Smith, got hold of Roberta Fenn and tried to pump her. When he didn't get anywhere, he came to us. He knew exactly what he wanted us to find out, but he wouldn't tip his hand. He sent us to New Orleans and told us to find Roberta Fenn, knowing that finding her would be a cinch. What he *really* wanted was to have us start investigating her past, get all the dope we could on her, and then talk with her. He thought that she might talk to someone who was trying to close up an estate where there was some money in it for her."

I said, "That could have been it all right."

"And because he handed us that song and dance," Bertha went on, "I made him a bedrock price. Oh, it was a price that had plenty of velvet, about two or three times what we'd have worked for in town, but—gosh, if I'd only known."

"You know now."

Bertha blinked at me and said, "That's right, I do."

I said, "Here's something else that happened."

"What?"

"I put Emory Hale in your apartment. He hadn't been there very long when he got to rummaging around in an old desk and found some clippings dealing with this murder of Howard Chandler Craig. It seems that Craig was riding with Roberta Fenn when the so-called love bandit stepped out of the bushes and took Craig's money and tried to take his girl. Craig wouldn't stand for it, and got shot. At least, that's the story the girl told."

"Go ahead," Bertha said. "Give me the rest of it."

I said, "In the bottom part of the desk was a thirty-eight caliber revolver. Craig was shot with a thirty-eight caliber bullet."

"Then Roberta Fenn was guilty of that murder. The story she told about the stick-up was all a lie."

"Not necessarily."

"Well, if it turns out that was the gun that committed the murder, it's a cinch that's right."

I shook my head.

"Why not?"

I said, "Hale got in touch with Roberta Fenn at a time when he was posing as Archibald C. Smith who was in the insurance business in Chicago. He tried to get Roberta to talk. Either she wouldn't talk or else she didn't talk the words Hale wanted to hear."

"What sort of words?" Bertha asked.

"That there was some collusion between her and Edna Cutler, that Edna knew of the filing of the divorce action, or anticipated a divorce action would be filed, and that papers would be served, and deliberately put Roberta Fenn in her apartment for the purpose of avoiding service."

"So then what?" Bertha asked.

I said, "Marco Cutler got a decree of divorce. He got an interlocutory decree, he didn't get his final. It's due. If Edna Cutler came into court, and had that interlocutory judgment set aside on the ground that she had known nothing about the action, and that summons had not been served upon her—now there's one other angle. If the thing was the other way around, we're being played for suckers."

"What do you mean?" Bertha asked.

"Suppose the whole thing is a beautiful frame-up. Suppose we're to appear in the role of giving it authenticity and a touch of first-class respectability."

"What do you mean?"

"Suppose Marco Cutler wanted to get a divorce. Suppose he knew that Edna Cutler would contest it. He didn't want to get in the midde of a contested divorce action because he himself was living in a glass house, and, therefore, wasn't able to throw stones. All right, he gets Roberta Fenn to go to New Orleans. She gets in touch with Edna Cutler. Edna is feeling pretty gloomy. Roberta skillfully plants in her mind the idea that it might be a swell stunt to disappear. Edna agrees. After the disappearance has been staged, Roberta passes the word on to Marco, and Marco gets his lawyers to file suit and send the papers to New Orleans for service. They serve Roberta as Edna Cutler. Edna actually never knows a single thing about the divorce action. They've wiped her off the slate without even giving her a chance."

"Then what?" Bertha asked.

I said, "Everything lies dormant until Edna finds out about it. Then just as she's getting ready to do something drastic, Hale comes to us on the theory that he wants us to find Roberta Fenn. We find her. Roberta is very coy. She arranges to be found at just the right time. In fact, if I hadn't found her by a process of detective work, she'd probably have stumbled into me on the street or dropped in at Jack O'Leary's Bar when I happened to be there."

"Go ahead," Bertha said. "All that stuff is so elemental there's no use wasting time on it. Give me the real lowdown."

I said, "The game was that we'd find Roberta. She'd get very, very friendly. She might even encourage me to make a pass at her. Then she'd 'tell me all,' only the 'all' would be that Edna Cutler certainly acted strangely about having her take her name. It would be just enough to indicate that there was a big frame-up on Edna's part to nick her husband. Edna would get thrown out of court."

"Pickle me for a peach!" Bertha said. "What are we going to do now, lover?"

"Absolutely nothing—not until we find out whether we're being played for suckers, or whether the whole thing is on the up and up."

"We've got to find Roberta Fenn."

"I have."

"Have what?"

"Found her."

"Where is she?"

I grinned at Bertha and said, "I've taken care of that little thing. You can search New Orleans from now until next year at this time and you'd never find her."

"Why?"

"I mean that I've hidden her, and this time I've made a good job of it."

"What's the idea of hiding her? Why not tell Hale that we've got her, and smoke the whole thing out into the open?"

"Then what?"

"Well, we'd—then we'd finish our contract."

"And where would that leave Roberta Fenn?"

"To hell with Roberta Fenn. I'm thinking about us."

"Think some more about us then."

"What do you mean?"

I said, "We're given a deck of marked cards. We're supposed to put them into the game—very innocently. All right, we put them into the game, collect our stipend, and that's all. But suppose we take the marked deck of cards, slip them into our pocket, forget to put them into the game, and a big jackpot is coming up? Then what?"

She gloated over me rapturously. "And I thought you were dumb about money matters!" For a moment I thought she was going to kiss me.

I got up and moved over toward the door.

"What do you want?" she asked.

I said, "I want you to sit in your office and not know

where I am. If Hale telephones, I've disappeared, too."

Bertha frowned. "I'd have to lie to him, wouldn't I?"

"You would now," I said. "If you hadn't been so smart about tracing telephone calls and hunting me up, you could have told him the truth—that you didn't know where I was."

"What are we going to do about that?" Bertha Cool asked.

I said, "When he rings up tonight, tell him you don't know *where* I am."

"You mean you want me to lie to him?"

I smiled at her and said, "No."

Bertha said, "What are you getting at?"

I said, "I want you to tell him the truth."

"I don't get you."

I held the door open for her. "By tonight," I told her, "you *won't* know where I am."

CHAPTER EIGHTEEN

I CAUGHT UP ON SLEEP for the biggest part of the afternoon. About six o'clock I tapped on the communicating door to Roberta's room.

"Yes," she called, "what is it?"

I opened the door a crack. "Getting hungry?"

"Come on in." She had a sheet pulled up over her. From the clothes on the chair, it looked as though the sheet was about all she had on.

She grinned, said, "This is my negligee. Donald, I've simply *got* to get some clothes. I've been using a purse as a suitcase and overnight bag until I feel like something the cat dragged in. The drugstore downstairs managed to give me enough creams, comb, brushes, and toilet articles, but no negligee."

I said, "I could use some clean clothes, but it's Sunday and the stores are closed."

"You live here, don't you? You must have a room with a lot of things in it."

"I have."

"Why don't you go get them?"

I smiled and shook my head.

"You think—that the police—"

"Yes."

"Donald, I'm sorry. I'm the one that got you into this mess."

"No, you didn't. It isn't any mess, and I'm not in it. I like the clothes I've got on."

She smiled. "Where would we go?"

"Oh, there are half a dozen places where we could get something to eat and perhaps do a little dancing."

"Donald, I'd *love* that."

"Okay, get your things on."

"Okay," she said. "I've washed out my undies and left them hanging in the bathroom. I think they're dry."

"How long?"

"Ten or fifteen minutes."

"Be seeing you."

I went back and closed the door, settled down and lit a cigarette. Fifteen minutes later she joined me, and thirty minutes after that we were seated in one of the less exclusive nightclubs with cocktails in front of us, and a special de luxe dinner ordered.

Getting a girl drunk is always a risky business. You don't know what she's going to do or what she's going to say when the cautiousness wears off and she gets right down to the real low-down. What's more, you never know whether you're not going to wake up with a terrific headache and find your victim has drunk you under the table.

I suggested a second cocktail. Roberta took it. She

turned me down on a third, but admitted that some wine would go nicely with the dinner.

I ordered sparkling Burgundy.

It was a place where people came to dine and talk, laugh, proposition, and be propositioned. Waiters made quite a show of bustling about, but didn't try to serve the dinners under an hour or an hour and a half.

Our dinner dragged into its second bottle of sparkling Burgundy, and I could see Roberta was getting tight. I was feeling pretty darn good myself.

"You never have told me what your partner said to you."

"Bertha?"

"Yes."

"That was because your delicate ears shouldn't hear such language."

"You'd be surprised at the things my delicate ears have heard. What's eating her?"

"Oh, just a general gripe."

She reached across the table. Her fingers closed around my hand. "You're protecting me, aren't you, Donald?"

"Perhaps."

"I knew you were. Your partner wanted you to find me and turn me in and you wouldn't do it. You had a fight about it. Isn't that right?"

"Listening at the door?" I asked.

Her eyes showed indignation. "Certainly not."

"Just general powers of deduction?"

She nodded slowly, with that serious solemnity which characterizes a woman who is saying to herself, *Now I'm pretty tight, but no one must know it. I'm going to nod my head, and I must be careful to see that it doesn't nod too far and fall right off in my lap.*

I said, "Bertha's all right now. You can forget about her. She was a little belligerent at first, but that doesn't mean anything—not with Bertha. She's like the camel, very even-tempered."

"Donald, suppose that *had* been the police. What could we have done?"

"Nothing."

"Suppose they pick me up. What am I to do?"

"Nothing."

"What do you mean?"

"Just that. Don't talk. Don't make any statements. Don't give them any information about anything until you've seen a lawyer."

"What lawyer?"

"I'll get you one."

"You're so good to me."

Her words were getting just a little thick. There was an effort in the concentration of her gaze, as if she wanted to be certain to hold me in one place so that I didn't drift out of her field of vision right while she was looking at me.

"Know something?" she asked abruptly.

"What?"

"I'm nuts about you."

"Forget it. You're cockeyed."

"I'm tight all right, but I'm still nuts about you. Didn't you know it back there in the hotel when I kissed you?"

"No, I didn't think anything about it."

Her eyes were large. "You should think something about it."

I leaned across the table, pushed the plates away to make a clear spot on the tablecloth. "Why did you leave Los Angeles?"

"Don't make me talk about it."

"I want to know."

The question seemed to sober her. She looked down at her plate, thought for a moment, said, "I could use a cigarette."

I gave her one and lit it.

"I'll tell you, if you make me, Donald, but I don't want to. You could make me do anything."

"I want to know, Rob."

"It was years ago, 1937."

"What happened?"

"I was out with a man in an automobile. We drove around just killing time, and then turned in to one of the parks, and—stopped."

"Necking?"

"Yes."

"Then what?"

"At that time they were having quite a bit of trouble with a love bandit, a chap who lay in wait in the places where the necking parties went on. I suppose you know the procedure."

"Holdup?"

"He'd take money from the men, and then—well, then he'd borrow the woman for a while."

"Go on."

"We were held up."

"What happened?"

"This man made a pass at me and my escort wouldn't stand for it. The bandit shot him—and got away."

"Were you suspected?"

"Suspected of what?" she asked, her eyes getting wide.

"Of having had anything to do with it."

"Good heavens, no. Everyone was just as sympathetic and nice to me as they could be. But—well, it clung to me. Of course, the people where I was working knew all about it. They'd keep talking about it. Once when I went out with a fellow one of the girls in the office didn't like she came to me and told me that a man had given his life in order to protect my honor, that I shouldn't hold it cheaply."

"What did you do?"

"I wanted to slap her face. All I could do was to smile and thank her.

"I quit my job, went to work in another place. In about two months they found out all about me. It was the same thing over and over. I suppose I'm just a damn heathen. I didn't love this man. I liked him. I was going with him off and on, but I was also going with some others. I had no intention of marrying him. If I'd known what he was going to do, I'd have stopped him. I didn't want him to give his life for me. It was a brave thing to do. It was a wonderful thing to do. It was so—so damned quixotic."

"I think it was what any man would have done under similar circumstances."

She smiled. "Statistics prove that you're wrong."

I knew she was right, so didn't say anything more.

"Well," she went on, "what with having all of my friends whispering around behind my back, and what with the memory of the tragedy gnawing at the back of my consciousness—I decided to travel. I went to New York. After a while I got a job as a model, advertising some lingerie. For a while things were all right, then people recognized my photographs. My friends started whispering again.

"I'd had a taste of complete freedom. It had lasted for almost a year. I knew what it was like to be just a common, average person, free to live my own life in my own way—"

"So you disappeared again?" I asked.

"Yes. I realized that I'd had the right idea but had made the mistake of getting into a profession where I was photographed. I decided to go to a new place, begin all over again, and smash the first camera that was pointed in my direction."

"New Orleans?"

"Yes."

"Then what?"

"You know the rest."

"How did you meet Edna Cutler?"

"I don't know now just how it was. I think it started in a cafeteria or a restaurant—it may have been the Bourbon House. Come to think of it, I guess it was.

That's something of a Bohemian place, you know. Most of the people who eat there regularly get to know the other people who eat there regularly. Quite a few of the prominent authors, playwrights, and actors eat there when in New Orleans. It's an unpretentious little place, but it has the atmosphere, the real, authentic, aged-in-the-wood brand."

"I know."

"Well, anyway, I got acquainted with her. I found out she was running away from something, too. She hadn't had as much of a success at it as I'd had, so I offered to take over her identity for a while and let her really disappear."

I said, "I'm anxious to get that straight, Rob. Did *you* make the offer to *her?*"

She thought for a moment and said, "Well, she paved the way for it. I guess it was her idea."

"You're certain?"

"Definitely, yes. Can I have another drink, Donald? You've made me get cold sober, talking about this thing. I didn't want to get sober tonight. I wanted to ring doorbells and have some fun."

I said, "There's a little more I want you to tell me first, little details about, for instance, when you first heard about Nostrander's death."

She said, "Put yourself in my position. One murder had been committed over me already. I was trying to dodge notoriety. Well, when this thing happened, I—I just acted on instinct. I wanted to run away from it."

"Not good enough, Rob," I told her.

"What isn't good enough?"

"That reason for running."

"It happens to be the truth."

I looked her straight in the eyes, said, "You know better, Rob. No one had thought you might have been implicated in the murder of that young man with whom you were riding back in 1937, but two murders in a girl's life are just too many murders. They'd begin to ask questions about that old murder, and they wouldn't be the same kind of questions they asked you five years ago."

"Honest, Donald, I never thought of that. But—well, I guess it's an angle to take into consideration. It's something to think of, all right."

"Let's go back to that love bandit. Did they ever catch him?"

"Yes."

"Did he confess?"

"Not to that crime. He always denied having had anything to do with that. He confessed to a couple of others."

"What did they do with him?"

"Hanged him."

"Did you ever see him?"

"Yes. They took me down to see if I could identify him."

"Could you?"

"No."

"Did you see him alone or in a line-up?"

"They showed him to me in a line-up, in one of those inspection boxes where a person stands on kind of a stage with a lot of lights beating on him and a white screen stretched across the front so he can't see you, and yet you can see him perfectly."

"And you couldn't pick him out of the line-up?"

"No."

"Then what did they do?"

"Then they put him in a darkened room where there was just a little light, put an overcoat and a hat on him, just the way he'd been dressed at the time of the crime, and asked me if I could identify him."

"Could you?"

"No."

"The man who killed your friend wore a mask?"

"Yes."

172

"Did you notice anything about him, anything at all?"

"Yes."

"What?"

"He walked with a limp when he came out of the bushes. After the shooting, when he ran away, he didn't limp."

"Did you tell the police that?"

"Yes."

"Did it mean anything to them?"

"I don't think so. Can't we quit talking about this and have a drink?"

I called the waiter over. "Same thing?" I asked her.

"I'm tired of wine. Could we have something else?"

"Two Scotch and sodas," I said. "How's that, Rob?"

"That's fine. And then do something for me, will you, Donald?"

"What?"

"Don't let me drink any more."

"Why?"

"I want to enjoy the night and not just get dizzy and a little sick and pass out and wake up in the morning with a head."

The waiter brought the drinks. I drank about half of mine, then excused myself and started in the general direction of the men's room. I detoured over to the telephone booth, got a couple of bills changed into twenty-five-cent pieces, and called Emory G. Hale at the hotel in New Orleans.

I had to wait less than three minutes while the operator put the call through; then I heard Hale's booming voice.

Central sweetly told me to start depositing twenty-five-cent pieces, and my quarters played a tune on the gong in the pay box.

It took a second or two for the sound of the gongs to get out of my ear. I heard Hale saying impatiently,

"Hello. Hello. Hello. Who is this calling? Hello."

"Hello, Hale. This is Donald Lam."

"Lam! Where are you?"

"Los Angeles."

"Well, why the devil didn't you report? I've been worried sick about you, wondering if you were all right."

"I'm all right. I've been too busy to get near a telephone. I've got Roberta Fenn located."

"You have?"

"Yes."

"Where?"

"Los Angeles."

"Bully for you! That's the way I like to have things done. No excuses. No alibis. Just results. You certainly are entitled—"

"You still have the key to that apartment?" I interrupted.

"Yes, of course."

I said, "All right. Roberta Fenn lived there. The landlady will identify her photograph. There was a flimflam on a divorce action. She was doubling for Edna Cutler. Edna Cutler lives at Shreveport in an apartment house that's called River Vista. She staked Roberta to the money to get out of New Orleans.

"Get in touch with Marco Cutler. You'll find him in one of the hotels in New Orleans. Tell him that Edna Cutler worked a clever scheme on him by trapping him into serving papers on a woman that wasn't the defendant. Tell him to come up and look over the apartment. When he does, be sure that *he* finds the gun and those old newspaper clippings. Then call in the police. Let the California authorities reopen that Craig murder case. As soon as you've done that, get on a plane and come to Los Angeles. I'll have Roberta Fenn all staked out for you."

Good nature bubbled out of him like coffee in an

electric percolator. "Lam, that's wonderful! Is Roberta Fenn in Los Angeles now?"

"Yes."

"Do you know where?"

"Yes."

"Where?"

"I'm shadowing her."

"Can you tell me exactly where she is?"

"Right at the present moment, she's in a nightclub. She's just getting ready to leave."

"Anyone with her?" he asked eagerly.

"Not at the moment."

"And you're not going to lose her?"

"I'm keeping an eye on her."

"That's splendid. Wonderful! Donald, you're a man in a million! When I said you were an owl, I really—"

Central interrupted to say, "Your three minutes are up."

"Good-by," I said, and slammed the receiver back onto its hook.

CHAPTER NINETEEN

THE ELEVATOR contained the usual Monday-morning crowd returning to the grind of routine office work, men who had gone without hats on the golf course or the beaches and whose foreheads were flaming with sunburn, girls looking a little weary about the eyes trying by intensive make-up to neutralize the telltale marks of not enough sleep—people who found the gloomy confines of an office doubly distasteful after a taste of a day spent in the open.

Elsie Brand was in the office ahead of me.

I could hear the machine-gun clatter of her typewriter as I approached the door marked *Cool and Lam, Confidential Investigations.*

She looked up as I entered the door. "Hello. Glad you're back. Have a nice trip?"

She swung around away from the typewriter, flashed a quick look at the clock as though determining how much of the partnership time she could afford to give to one of the partners.

"So-so."

"Did a good job on that Florida case, didn't you?"

"It turned out all right."

"How's the New Orleans business?"

"Hanging fire. Where's Bertha?"

"Hasn't come in yet."

"Did she make some investigation in that Roxberry Estates matter?"

"Uh huh. There's a file—quite a few notes."

She got up from the chair, crossed over to the filing cases, ran her finger down the index, jerked open a drawer in the steel file, stabbed at the pasteboard jackets with the swift certainty of one who knows exactly what she is doing, pulled out a file, and handed it to me.

"You'll find in there everything we've been able to get."

"Thanks. I'll take a look at it. How's the construction business coming along?"

She glanced quickly at the door, lowered her voice, and said, "There's been a bit of correspondence about the business. It's all in the file. Some of the other correspondence is in Bertha's office—locked up. She hasn't sent it out to the file. I don't know where it is."

"What's that correspondence about?"

"Getting you placed in a deferred classification."

"Did she make it stick?"

Again Elsie looked at the door. "This would cost me my job if she knew about it."

"Don't I have something to say about that?"

"Not about that. She'd ride me so I had to quit."

"Well, what about it? Did she fix it up?"

"Yes."

"When?"

"Last week."

"It's all settled?"

"Yes."

I said, "Thanks."

She watched me curiously. A puzzled frown appeared between her arched eyebrows. "Are you going to let her get away with it?"

"Sure."

"Oh."

"What did you expect me to do?" I asked.

"Nothing," she said, without looking up.

I took the file of the Roxberry Estates into my private office, sat down at the desk, and went over it in detail.

It told me nothing.

Silas T. Roxberry had done a lot of financing, putting money in various business activities, some of which he controlled, some of which were simply outlets for funds which he held for business investment. He had died in 1937, leaving two children, a son named Roy aged fifteen, a daughter named Edna aged nineteen. Because his affairs had been considerably complicated and a distribution of the estate might have resulted in a shrinkage of assets, it had been decided to assign the rights of the heirs to a corporation known as Roxberry Estates and a decree of distribution had been made to the corporation, the heirs taking stock in that corporation to the extent of their interests.

Howard C. Craig had been Roxberry's confidential bookkeeper, had been employed by him for nearly seven years. The Roxberry Estates Corporation employed Craig as its secretary and treasurer. After Craig's death, a man named Sells had taken Craig's place. An attorney by the name of Biswill had handled the estate and had become general manager of the corporation. He was carrying on the business in just about the same way that Silas Roxberry had. Because it was a closed corporation, it was impossible to learn anything about the degree of success with which the business was being administered, but Bertha Cool had secured a commercial report to the effect that the business was solvent, prompt in paying its bills, although it was rumored it had, of late, made some poor investments.

It was, of course, possible that Edna Roxberry was Edna Cutler. I picked up the telephone, got the Roxberry Estates on the phone, said I was a friend of the family who had been away for several years, and asked if Edna Roxberry was married. I was told she hadn't married as yet and I would find her name in the telephone book. The party at the other end of the line wanted to know who was talking, and I hung up.

At ten o'clock Bertha still hadn't showed up.

I told Elsie I was going out, and went over to the offices of the Roxberry Estates.

It was possible to tell the whole story in the lettering on the doors of the offices. Originally Harman C. Biswill had had a string of offices. Silas Roxberry had been one of his main clients. With Roxberry's death, Biswill had moved in on the estate. Having sold the heirs on the idea of making distribution to a corporation, he had become the manager of the corporation. Now, the signs on the doors read, *Harman C. Biswill, Attorney at Law. Private. Entrance 619,* and on 619 appeared *Roxberry Estates, Inc. Entrance.* Down below in the left-hand corner was *Harman C. Biswill, Attorney at Law. Entrance.* The lettering on the door of the private office looked rather faded. It had been Biswill's old private office, and he hadn't changed the sign. As he'd gradually abandoned the general practice of law for the more profitable gravy of the estate corporation, he'd changed the sign on the entrance room.

It didn't take a first-class detective to tell that Harman C. Biswill had cut himself a very nice slice of cake.

I opened the entrance door and walked in.

Biswill had gone hog wild on office machinery. There were bookkeeping machines, typewriters, dictating machines, adding machines, billing machines, addressing machines scattered around the office. An elderly woman was punching an adding machine. A girl was pounding out correspondence on a typewriter, the earpieces of a transcribing machine dangling from her ears.

There was a switchboard and a little window marked *Information,* but no one was at the desk. As I came in, a light came on on the switchboard and a buzzer sounded. The woman at the adding machine came over to the switchboard, plugged in a line, said, "Roxberry Estates, Incorporated. . . . No, he isn't here. . . . I can't tell you just when he will be. . . . No, I'm not certain he'll be here at all today. . . . Was there any message? . . . Very well, I'll tell him. . . . Thank you."

She was past fifty, a woman who had evidently been working all of her life. Her eyes were tired but kind, and there was about her the air of a person who knows exactly what she is doing.

I followed a hunch. "You've been with the corporation since it was organized?"

"Yes."

"And were employed by Mr. Roxberry prior to that time?"

"Yes. What is it you wish?"

I said, "I'm trying to find out something about a man by the name of Hale."

"What did you want to know about him?"

"Something about his credit."

"May I have your name?"

"Lam. Donald Lam."

"And what company are you with, Mr. Lam?"

"It's a partnership," I said. "Cool and Lam. I'm one of the partners. We're doing some business with Mr. Hale."

"Just a moment, and I'll see what I can find out."

She went into the back part of the office, opened a card index, ran down through a number of cards, pulled out one, looked at it, and returned to the counter.

"What were the initials?"

"Mr. Hale's?"

"Yes."

"Emory G. Hale. He may have been an attorney when he was here."

She looked at the card again, said, "We have no Emory G. Hale. No record of ever having done business with him."

I said, "Perhaps you can remember him. He may have been representing someone else, and it's possible you didn't have his name, a tall man around six feet. He's about fifty-seven or fifty-eight years of age, has broad shoulders and very long arms. When he smiles, he has a peculiar habit of holding his front teeth together and pulling back his lips."

She thought for a minute, shook her head, and said, "I'm afraid I'm not able to help you. We carried on rather a large and varied business. Mr. Roxberry did both personal and business financing."

"Yes, I know. And you don't remember Mr. Hale?"

"No."

"He might even have been going under another name."

"No. I'm quite certain."

I started for the door, turned back suddenly, and said, "Did you have business dealings with a Marco Cutler?"

She shook her head.

"Or," I asked almost as an afterthought, "an Edna Cutler?"

"Edna P. Cutler?" she asked.

"I believe that's right."

"Oh, yes, we had quite a large number of dealings with Edna Cutler."

"Do those dealings continue?"

"No. They were all wound up. Mr. Roxberry did a lot of business for Miss Cutler."

"Miss or Mrs.?"

She frowned and said, "I don't know. I only remember the name on the books as Edna P. Cutler."

"What did you call her when she came in?" I asked. "Miss or Mrs.?"

"I don't think I ever saw her in my life."

"Her account isn't active now?"

"Oh, no. It was some sort of a joint deal she had with Mr. Roxberry. Just a minute. Frances," she called to the girl at the transcribing machine, "hasn't all the Edna Cutler business been closed up?"

The girl stopped typing long enough to nod her head, and then went back to the typewriter.

The woman behind the counter gave me a tired smile of dismissal.

I went out and stood in the corridor, thinking.

Edna Cutler. Many business dealings with Silas Roxberry. . . . Yet she never came to the office. . . . Howard Chandler Craig, a bookkeeper. . . . Out riding with Roberta Fenn. . . . A mysterious love pirate, and the bookkeeper of the Roxberry Estates, the one who must have had all the financial transactions of Silas T. Roxberry at his finger tips, murdered.

I rang up the office, found that Bertha Cool hadn't come in yet, told Elsie Brand I would be in around noon, and if Bertha came in, to tell her to wait.

I went down to police headquarters.

Sergeant Pete Rondler of the Homicide Squad had

always got a kick out of me. For one reason, he had had a couple of run-ins with Bertha Cool, and hated the ground she walked on. When I started working for her, he'd predicted I'd be a thoroughly broken-in doormat within three months. The fact that I'd worked up to a partnership and that, on occasion, I stood up to Bertha Cool gave him a great deal of private satisfaction.

"Hello, Sherlock," he said as I opened the door. "Want something?"

"Maybe."

"How's the sleuthing?"

"Only fair."

"How are you and Bertha getting along?"

"Swell."

"Don't see any footprints on your hip pockets."

"Not yet."

"She'll get you in time. You can stall her off for a while, but you're just living on borrowed time. She'll earmark you, put her brand on you, kid you along until you're fattened up, and then send you to the slaughterhouse. After she has your hide nicely tanned and made into leather, she'll start looking for another victim."

"That's where I fool her," I said. "I won't get fat."

He grinned. "What's on your mind?"

"Nineteen-thirty-seven. Unsolved murder. Man by the name of Howard Chandler Craig."

He had bushy eyebrows. When he frowned, they came down over his eyes like black thunderclouds piling up behind a mountain. Now I got the full effect of them.

"Aren't you funny?" he said.

"I didn't think I was being funny."

"What do you know about that?"

"Nothing."

"When were you in New Orleans?"

I hesitated.

"Start lying to me," he said, "and I'll bust your damn

agency. You won't get a bit of co-operation as long as you live."

"I just got back from there."

"I thought so."

"Why, what's wrong?"

He placed his forearm flat on the desk, raised the wrist, and slapped the tips of his fingers with an up-and-down drumming motion against the scarred desk top. At length, he said, "The New Orleans police are making inquiries."

"There may be a New Orleans angle on it."

"What?"

I looked him straight in the eye, said with wide-eyed candor, "A girl by the name of Roberta Fenn was riding in the car with Craig when he was killed. She's been mixed up in another murder case in New Orleans. Police aren't certain what happened, whether she was a victim or whether she pulled the trigger, or whether she's just got frightened and taken a powder."

"Two murders in five years is altogether too many murders for a nice young girl."

"So it would seem."

"What's your angle on the case?"

"Just investigating."

"For whom?"

"A lawyer," I said, "trying to close up an estate."

"Nuts!"

"That's the truth. That's what he's told us anyway."

"Who's the lawyer?"

I grinned.

"What's the angle?"

"We're looking for a person who seems to have disappeared."

"Oh."

Rondler pulled a cigar from his pocket, puckered his lips as though he were going to whistle, but he didn't whistle. He simply made little blowing noises as he carefully clipped off the end of the cigar. Then, as he pulled a match from his pocket, he said, "Okay, here's the dope. Around the latter part of 1936 we were troubled with a man who stuck up petting-parties. He'd take whatever the man had, and if the girl was good-looking, he'd take her, too. It made quite a stink. We put men out and staged mock petting-parties and did our damnedest to bait a trap he'd walk into. Nothing doing.

"When it began to get cold and people didn't sit out in automobiles and neck so much, our bandit suddenly quit. We thought we were rid of him; but in the spring of '37 when things began to warm up, our petting-party bandit was right back again.

"Several guys put up a squawk when he started to take their women. This bird Craig was one of them. There were three altogether. Two of them were killed. One was shot, and recovered. Things got pretty serious. The chief told us to get this bird, or else.

"We kept baiting traps. He wouldn't walk into them. Then somebody got the bright idea. A guy who does that sort of stuff doesn't do it and then lay off, and then do it again. It's a steady racket with him. So why did he lay off during the cold months? Of course, the pickings were rather slim, but there were pickings just the same, and logically you'd have thought he'd have been easier to trap when he didn't have so much to choose from.

"So we got the idea perhaps he'd gone some place else for the winter months. San Diego was all clear. So we looked up Florida. Sure enough, back of Miami there'd been a lot of trouble with a petting-party bandit during the winter of '36 and '37. What's more, they had a couple of clues, some fingerprints, and something we could work on.

"That gave us an opportunity. We figured this man was driving an automobile that was registered in California. We thought that he was a lone wolf, particularly that he had no woman. It was a tedious job, but we started checking the license numbers of California vehicles that had been registered in Florida, of California vehicles that had crossed through the state quarantine inspection station at Yuma in the two weeks before the first petting-party holdup took place in Los Angeles.

"That gave us our first clue. We found a car registered to a man named Rixmann had crossed at Yuma just four days before the first of our spring petting-party holdups in '37. We looked Rixmann up. He was rather good-looking in a dark, sullen sort of way. He'd been out of work for some time. His landlady didn't know just what he did. He seemed to be moody and morose, but paid his rent on time, had plenty of money, and slept a lot during the day. He drove a Chevrolet coupé and stored it in a garage back of the place where he roomed. Two or three nights a week he'd go to a picture show, but a couple of nights a week he'd take his car and go out. She'd hear him come back quite late. All this was in the late summer of '37.

"Of course, on these petting-party holdups where there's an assault on the girl, it's only about one out of four or five that makes a complaint to the police. Sometimes the man can't afford to have his name put on the police records. Sometimes the woman can't. Sometimes when there's rape, the woman feels that it's poor business to make a complaint and have the newspapers publish all the facts."

"Was it Rixmann?" I asked.

"That was the bird we wanted," Rondler said. "We started shadowing him, and about the third night he took his car down to one of the lovers' lanes, parked it, got out and walked about three hundred yards, waited where it was good and dark under a tree. That gave us all we needed. We had a woman police investigator who was willing to go through with it. We caught Rixmann red-handed—and I mean we really caught him. Of course, the boys worked him over some, and when he arrived here in this office, he was all softened up.

"He sat right over there in that chair and spilled his guts. He knew it was curtains for him. Right at the time, he didn't care. Afterward he got a lawyer and tried to plead insanity. He didn't make it stick. He told us that he had a very fine pair of night binoculars. He picked places where he could wait in the dark, but where there was a little light that would shine on the spot where cars would naturally be parked. He'd look occupants over with his night binoculars, and study them carefully before he went out to make his holdup. Three or four times he'd seen a couple of policemen stage a mock petting-party, and he sat watching them through his binoculars and getting a great kick out of it. With those night glasses, you couldn't fool him. He knew it was a trap, and simply stayed there in the dark and outwaited them.

"He told the story. He couldn't remember all the jobs he'd pulled, but he could remember enough of them. He remembered the shootings, of course. He always did swear he didn't pull off that Craig job. Some of the other boys didn't believe him. I did. I couldn't see why he'd lie about that when he was talking his neck into a noose, anyway."

"Did they hang him?"

"Gas," Rondler said. "By the time they got him convicted, he had grown surly. He never would talk after that first night. He got hold of a lawyer, and the lawyer told him to clam up. They pleaded insanity, and they tried to keep that pose right up to the moment of execution, thinking perhaps he'd get a reprieve. I never have felt, though, that the Craig case was closed."

"What's your idea?" I asked him.

"I haven't any. I don't have enough facts to work on, *but* I'll tell you what it could have been."

"What?"

"That Fenn girl could have been crazy about him. She wanted him to marry her, and he wouldn't. She tried all the old gags, and they didn't work. He was in

186

love with somebody else and was going to get married. She took him out for a last petting party, made an excuse to get out of the car, walked around on the driver's side, pulled the trigger, ditched the gun, and ran down the road screaming. It was that simple."

I said, "That could have been it all right."

"Most of the murders that people get away with are just like that," Sergeant Rondler went on. "They're so damn simple that they're foolproof. There's nothing about them to go haywire. The more people plan, the more elaborately they try to work out something that will cheat the law, the more they leave a lot of loose threads they haven't thought about and which can't be tied up. The bird who commits the successful crime is the one who just has one main thread. He ties that in a good, tight square knot, then walks away and leaves it."

I said, "How about that Craig murder? Any fingerprints or anything to go on?"

"Absolutely nothing except a description given by Roberta Fenn."

"What was that?"

He opened the drawer of his desk, grinned, and said, "I just had it brought in after we got that wire from New Orleans. She describes the chap as being medium size, wearing a dark suit, an overcoat, a felt hat, and a mask. She says he was *not* wearing gloves, that when he first appeared on the scene, he limped noticeably, that when he ran away, he didn't limp. Hell of a description."

"Could you have done any better if you'd been there?"

He grinned. "Probably not. But if Rixmann didn't pull that job, she did."

"What makes you think so?"

"It's a cinch. That's the only petting-party job that isn't accounted for. After Rixmann was arrested, they quit as though you'd sliced them off with a knife. If someone else had been muscling in on Rixmann's racket, we'd have had more of the same."

I pushed back my chair, said, "You'd better light that cigar before you chew it to death."

I saw his eyebrows come together again. "You're getting a hell of a lot of information without giving much."

"Perhaps I haven't much to give."

"And then again, perhaps you have. Listen, Donald, I'm going to tell you something."

"What?"

"If you're playing around with that woman, we're going to nail you."

"What woman?"

"Roberta Fenn."

"What about her?"

"The police in New Orleans want her, and the way things are now, so do we."

"What's the next paragraph?"

"If you know where she is and are keeping her under cover, you're going to get a spanking right where it's going to hurt, and it's going to be a nice, hard spanking."

I said, "Okay, thanks for the tip," and walked out.

From a booth in the building, I called the office. Bertha Cool had just come in. I told her I'd be there in about two hours. She wanted to know what was doing, and I told her I couldn't discuss it over the telephone.

I went to the hotel. Roberta Fenn was sleeping late. I sat on the edge of her bed, said, "Let's talk."

"Okay."

"This man Craig. What about him?"

"I was going with him."

"Did you perhaps want to marry him, and he wouldn't marry you?"

"No."

"Were you in trouble?"

"No."

"You knew the people he was working for?"

"Yes. Roxberry, and after Roxberry died, the Roxberry Estates."

"Did he ever talk to you about the business affairs of the company?"

"No."

I held her eyes. "Did he ever mention Edna Cutler?"

"No."

I said, "You could be lying, you know."

"Why, Donald?"

"If you and Edna Cutler were teamed up together and if perhaps the two of you framed that deal up on Marco Cutler, you might find yourself facing two murder raps instead of one."

"Donald, I've told you the truth about that."

"You didn't have any idea papers were going to be served on you as Edna Cutler?"

"Absolutely not. I didn't know where Edna was, I tell you. I just went in there and took her name the way we agreed, and—"

"I know," I told her. "You've gone all over that before."

I got up off the bed.

"Where are you going?"

"I'm working."

She said, "I'm going to get some breakfast, and then go down and buy a few clothes. I feel awfully naked without a nightgown."

I said, "You'd better stay off the streets. Have your meals served up here. Get whatever things you want in the department store across the street. Don't do any telephoning, and no matter what you do, don't try to communicate with Edna Cutler."

"Why should I try to communicate with her?"

"I don't know. I'm just telling you not to."

"I won't, Donald. I promise. I won't do anything you don't want me to."

I said, "We're coming back to that murder case."

The expression on her face showed how she felt about it.

"I'm sorry, but I've got to take it up again. That masked figure that came walking toward the car wearing an overcoat was limping?"

"Yes."

"When he ran away, he didn't limp?"

"That's right."

"The figure was medium-sized?"

"Well, yes. Rather—I've thought that over a lot since then. I was excited you know at the time—but without the overcoat, I think he'd have been rather slender."

I said, "Okay, think this one over. Could it have been a woman?"

"A woman! Why, the man tried to make me! He—"

"All right," I interrupted. "That's part of the gag. Could it have been a woman?"

She frowned, said, "Of course, the overcoat concealed the figure. He was wearing pants and man's shoes, but—"

"*Could* it have been a woman?"

"Why, yes," she said, "of course it could. But then he tried to make me go with him. He—"

I said, "That's all. Forget about it. You're certain Craig never said anything to you about Edna Cutler?"

"Why, no. I don't know that he knew her. Did he?"

"I don't know. I'm asking you."

"He never said anything."

I said, "Okay, be good. Be seeing you for dinner. 'By."

CHAPTER TWENTY

THE MAN at the Navy Recruiting Office didn't ask a lot of questions. He just hit the high spots and gave me a questionnaire to fill out. When I had the blanks all filled in, he looked it over, said, "When do you want your physical examination?"

"How soon can I have it?"

"Now if you want it."

"I want it now."

I was escorted into a back room and relieved of my clothes. They gave me the works—and passed me.

"How much time do you want to get your business straightened up?"

"Twenty-four hours?" I asked.

"Okay. Be back here at one o'clock Tuesday afternoon, ready to go."

I told him I'd be there, and drove up to the agency office. Bertha was fuming with impatience.

"Where the hell have you been?" she demanded.

"I was in a couple of times during the morning, but you weren't here, so I had to go ahead on my own."

Her eyes were snapping. "What have you been doing now, wrecking the business, I suppose?"

"I hope not."

She handed me a wire.

Congratulations to your owl. Arriving eight-thirty plane. Meet me airport.

The signature was *Emory G. Hale.*

"I know," I said. "I telephoned him."

"What did you telephone him?"

"That I'd found Roberta Fenn."

"I thought you said not to tell him."

"No. It's all right to tell him that."

Bertha said, "The afternoon papers have headlines, *Solution of New Orleans murder sought here.* The paper says police are looking for Roberta Fenn. They've dug up the stuff about her being mixed up in the murder of Howard Chandler Craig, the guy who was killed by Rixmann, the petting-party bandit."

"Uh huh."

"You don't seem surprised."

"No."

"Trying to pump you for information," Bertha said angrily, "is a hopeless task. You have to pour in more than you can hope to take out. What I'm trying to tell you is that she's hot. If you know where she is, or if you've hid her out, you're going to get your fingers burned."

"How's the war-construction business coming along?"

Instantly Bertha went on the defensive. Her aggressive manner disappeared. She was suavely polite. "Bertha's going to have to talk with you about that, lover."

"What about it?"

"If anyone should ask you any questions, remember that while you aren't familiar with the details, you're the big executive. Bertha hasn't been feeling well lately. I think it's her heart, and she's got to rely more and more on you. Bertha signed this contract. There's some money in it, if we watch things carefully and don't let those carpenters slip things over on us. But you've got to take over most of the management."

"On account of your heart?" I asked.

"Yes."

"I didn't know it was bothering you."

"I didn't either until all the strain and excitement caught up with me. I don't think it's anything serious, but it bothers me."

"How?"

"Palpitation after eating."

"Have you seen a doctor?"

"And I get short of breath sometimes."

"Did you go to a doctor?"

"When I lie down, I can feel my heart pounding so it shakes the whole bed."

"But the question is, did you go to a doctor?"

"Hell, no!" Bertha exclaimed angrily. "Why would I want to go to a swivel-eyed sawbones and have him carve me all up at so much a slice?"

"I just thought a doctor might help."

"Well, he wouldn't."

"Sometime you might want to get a physician's certificate."

"When I do, I'll get one all right. Don't you worry about that."

"What am I supposed to do about this construction job?"

"Bertha will have to go over it with you, lover. Let's try and get this case finished first. But if anyone should start asking questions, remember that I haven't been able to stand the strain, that I'm threatened with a breakdown, and you're taking over the entire construction."

"But why should I say that?"

Bertha said angrily, "Dammit, don't be so contrary. Say it because—" She caught herself, after a moment finished in a more conversational tone of voice: "because you wouldn't want to let Bertha down, particularly when Bertha had bitten off more than she could chew trying to do something for her country."

"Patriotism?" I asked.

"We've *all* got to do our part," Bertha said unctuously.

I said, "All right, do you want to meet Hale with me?"

"Do you think I should?"

"Yes."

"All right, lover, whatever you say."

I stretched, yawned. "Well, I have a few odds and ends to do. I'll meet you here at seven-forty-five on the dot."

"I'll be here," Bertha promised. "I want to wait for the afternoon mail. I'm expecting a package. When it comes, I'll show you something. You'll see Bertha's a smart buyer. Merchandise you can't get any more, and I'm getting it cheap—real silk hosiery. You'll be surprised."

I went to the public library and put in the rest of the afternoon reading an old file of newspapers—the ones that dealt with all the activities of the petting-party stick-up man—and I paid particular attention to the Craig case.

I came out about 5:30 and started for the hotel, but stopped at a shoe-shine place on Fifth Street. I picked up an afternoon paper and settled down to read while my shoes were being shined.

I turned to the personals.

Rob. Am here in Los Angeles. Must talk with you at once. Regardless of what anyone has told you, I have your interests at heart. Telephone Helman 6-9544 and ask for me. Edna C.

The shoe shine was just about finished. I surprised him by jumping down off the stool, flipping him a quarter, and saying, "That's all we need for now."

A taxi rushed me to the hotel. I got my key and went up to the room.

The maid had been in. The rooms were made. Roberta wasn't there. She had evidently gone shopping, because a very thin peach-colored nightgown lay on the bed, together with two pairs of stockings of about the same shade. There was a paper package on the foot of the bed, and a smart compact traveling-bag on a chair. The traveling-bag was empty. The price tag was still on it. A newspaper lay on the floor.

I went back to my room, picked up the receiver, and said to the girl at the switchboard, "My sister telephoned a friend and went out to meet her. She gave me the telephone number and I've lost it. Can you look at the records and tell me the last number that was called from this room?"

"Just a moment."

I waited for about ten seconds; then she gave it to me: "Helman six—nine-five-four-four."

I said, "That's the number. Ring it back, will you, please?"

I waited on the line, heard the connection being made; then a voice said, "Palm View Hotel."

"You have an Edna Cutler of New Orleans registered?" I asked.

"Just a moment."

Another five seconds, and I had the information. Miss Cutler had checked out about twenty minutes earlier. She had left no forwarding address.

I hung up the telephone, took the elevator down to the lobby, went into a luggage store, bought a suitcase, went back upstairs, threw all of my belongings into the suitcase. I packed the paper parcel on Roberta's bed without unwrapping it. I also put in her nightgown and stockings. The creams and toilet articles on the dresser I managed to get into the little bag she'd purchased.

I moistened a towel and went over the place for fingerprints, rubbing door handles, mirrors, dresser tops—anything I thought she might have touched. When I had finished I telephoned the office to send up someone for the baggage. I went down and checked out, telling the clerk that my mother had passed away very suddenly, and that my sister and I were going out to stay with another sister who lived in Venice and was completely broken up. We didn't want to leave her alone.

I took a taxicab to the Union Depot, let it go, checked the baggage, put the checks in a stamped envelope, scribbled my office address on the outside, sealed the envelope, and dropped it into the mailbox. I looked at my watch and saw I had just time to go down to the office, pick up Bertha Cool, and get out to the airport.

CHAPTER TWENTY-ONE

THE PLANE CAME ROARING DOWN out of the sky, to soar along for a few feet, skimming the ground; then the wheels touched the cement runway, and the big transcontinental express glided slowly to a landing, then snarled into speed as it came up the runway and swung gracefully around in a wide pivot, stopping almost directly in front of the exit gate.

Emory G. Hale was the second one off. He was talking with a rather distinguished-looking individual who wore a close-cropped, gray mustache, half spectacles, and looked altogether too much like a banker to be a banker.

Hale seemed in a rare good humor as though he had had a wonderful trip. When he saw us he came toward us with outstretched hand, his face wreathed in his characteristic set smile.

His greeting for Bertha was hurried. Most of his attention was for me.

"Lam, I'm certainly glad to see you! I was hoping that you'd get down here to meet the plane. That's splendid of you. Lam, I want you to meet—but pardon, me, I'm forgetting my manners. Mrs. Cool, may I present Lieutenant Pellingham of the New Orleans police force? And this is Donald Lam, Lieutenant."

We all shook hands.

Hale seemed to be enjoying his role of master of

ceremonies. "Lieutenant Pellingham is an expert on ballistics. He does most of the technical work for the New Orleans Police Department. He's brought that gun with him, Lam. I told him that you were with me when we first discovered the weapon, that we debated whether we should call in the police at once, or wait until you had made an investigation in Los Angeles to get the exact status of the Craig murder case."

Hale glanced significantly at me as though trying to impress upon me that this preliminary speech was my cue to follow along, and not make any contradictory statements.

I nodded at Lieutenant Pellingham, said, "I've already been in touch with Sergeant Rondler here in headquarters."

"You didn't tell him about the gun?" Hale asked.

I seemed surprised. "The gun! Why, no! I understood I was simply to investigate the murder, and then if it appeared the crime had been committed with a thirty-eight caliber revolver which had never been found, I was to get in touch with you, and you were to notify the police."

"That's right," Hale said, positively beaming at me. "That's exactly the way I understood it. But," he went on, "you were with me when I first discovered the gun there in the desk. That's the point that Lieutenant Pellingham was interested in. He wants some corroborating evidence."

I turned to the lieutenant. "Mr. Hale was looking through the desk. There were some papers which had evidently dropped down in a partition behind a desk drawer. When we started to get them out, we discovered a revolver."

"You can identify that revolver, of course?" Lieutenant Pellingham asked.

I said, "It was a thirty-eight, blued-steel. I'm not certain of the make of the gun. It—"

Pellingham said, "That's not the point. What I'm

getting at is that you can identify *the gun which you saw there.*"

I looked at him blankly. "Why, I can tell you the general kind of a gun it was."

"But you can't tell me whether the gun I have is the *same* gun?"

"Of course it's the same," Hale said.

I hesitated; then after a moment I said, "Of course, neither one of us jotted down the serial numbers or any thing of that sort. We simply saw this gun there in the desk, but we put it back where we found it, and if Hale says it's the same gun, that's good enough for me."

"Of course it's the same gun," Hale said. "I can assure you on that point."

Pellingham said, "What we need is someone who can assure a jury."

"Oh, we can do that all right," Hale said confidently.

I said to Pellingham, "If you have this gun with you, perhaps I can identify it. If I can, it might be a good idea for me to scratch my initials on it."

Pellingham said, "That's an excellent idea. And when you get on the witness stand, you won't need to tell anyone when those initials were scratched on it. Do you get me?"

"I'm not certain that I do."

"The district attorney will simply say, 'Mr. Lam, I show you a gun which has scratched on it the initials D.L. I'll ask you who scratched those initials on there, if you know.' Then you'll say, 'I did.' Then the district attorney will say, 'Why?' and you'll say, 'So I could identify it.' Then the district attorney will ask you, 'Is this the revolver which you first saw in a desk in an apartment in New Orleans?' and so on, and so on."

I said, "I see."

"That's splendid," Hale said. "We'll both scratch our initials on there."

Pellingham took us over to a corner of the waiting-room. "We'll do it right here," he said, "because I'm going to rush right up to police headquarters, fire some test bullets, and compare them with the fatal bullet which killed young Craig."

We watched him while he placed a light Gladstone bag on his lap, opened it, took out a small wooden box. He slid the cover back on this wooden box. Tied to the bottom by strings which went through holes bored in the wood was the .38 caliber revolver the agency had furnished me months earlier.

Hale pounced on it. "That's the one," he said emphatically. "That's the one that was in there. And I'm betting ten to one it was the gun that killed this man Craig."

"Scratch your initials on it," Pellingham said and handed him a knife.

Hale scratched his initials on the rubber butt plate of the revolver.

Pellingham handed the gun to me.

I looked at it carefully. "I *think* it's the same gun. Of course, I didn't take down the serial number. But as nearly as I can tell—"

Hale said, "Why, Lam! Of course it's the gun. You know that."

"I *think*—well, it looks—"

Pellingham said, "Here, put your initials on it." He handed me his knife.

Bertha was looking from the gun to me. Her face was a study. Hale was beaming.

Pellingham said, "Now you've identified that gun. Don't go back on that identification, and don't let any shyster lawyer mix you up when he comes to the cross-examination."

The loud-speaker blared, "Telegram for Lieutenant Pellingham of New Orleans police force. Inquire at the ticket office, Lieutenant, please."

Pellingham said, "Excuse me," and closed the Gladstone. He went to the ticket window.

Hale said, "I'm glad you identified that gun, Lam.

We should have taken the serial number when we first found it."

Bertha said, "I'm surprised you didn't think of that, Donald."

Hale laughed. "He's a wise owl all right, Mrs. Cool, but even an owl blinks once in a while. This is the one slip he's made, and—"

Bertha interrupted. looking hard at me, "Owls don't blink."

Pellingham came hurrying toward us, a telegram in his hand, his lips tight. "Lam, did you take a plane from Fort Worth Saturday night?"

"Why?" I asked.

"Did you?"

"Yes."

"All right, Lam. I'm going to ask you to go to head-quarters with me—at once."

I said, "I'm sorry. I've got other things to do. They're important."

"I don't give a damn what you've got to do. You're coming with me."

"Got any authority for that?"

Pellingham's hand dropped down to his side trousers pocket. I thought he was going to come out with a star. Instead he brought out a nickel.

"See that?" he asked. "That's my authority."

"Five cents' worth?"

"No. When I drop that nickel into the coin box of a pay telephone and call police headquarters, I'll have all the authority I need to back up anything I want to do."

I felt Hale's eyes burning into mine, saw Bertha's glittering stare of intense concentration, and the fixed, cold-blooded determination of Pellingham's gray eyes.

"Are you going to come with me now?" Pellingham asked.

I said, "Go ahead and drop your nickel," and started for the door.

Bertha Cool and Emory Hale stood completely petri-

fied, looking at me as though I'd dropped a mask and
turned out to be a stranger.

Pellingham took it all as a matter of course. He might
have been expecting that particular development in
that particular way, from the minute he had opened
the interview. He marched calmly and without hurry
toward a telephone booth.

The agency car was outside. I jumped in it and made
time. I had to make a detour to be safe, up through
Burbank to Van Nuys, then down to Ventura Boulevard, then through Sepulveda to Wilshire Boulevard,
and into Los Angeles that way. I knew that Pellingham
would have the other roads blocked by officers and a
description of the agency car out.

CHAPTER TWENTY-TWO

I DIDN'T HAVE TIME to bury the agency car. I simply
drove it into a parking lot near the Palm View Hotel
and left it.

I went into the hotel, found the bell captain, and
pulled a couple of dollars from my pocket.

"Something I can do for you?" he asked.

"I want about two dollars' worth of information."

"Shoot."

"Sometime early this afternoon a woman who was
registered here as Edna Cutler checked out."

"Lots of women check out."

"You'll remember this one because she's brunette and
has a figure."

"I seem to remember her checking in. I don't remember her checking out."

"She wouldn't have had much baggage. There was another girl with her, a brunette with hazel eyes. She wore a black dress with a red belt, a red hat, and—"

"I get you now. They got Jeb Miller's cab."

"Know where I could find him?"

"He should be outside now. He has a regular stand here."

I handed the bellboy the two dollars. He said, "Come on, and I'll introduce you to Miller."

Jeb Miller listened to what I had to say. He squinted his eyes in an attempt to cudgel his memory into line. "Yeah, I remember the two dames," he said. "I'm trying to remember where I took them. It was a little apartment house somewhere out on Thirty-fifth Street. I can't remember the number. I could take you out there and—"

I had the cab door open before he realized he was getting a passenger.

"Don't pay any attention to speed limits," I told him.

"Says who?" he asked. "An officer?"

I pulled out my wallet. "Says the bankroll."

"Okay."

We started with a jerk. The signal at the corner changed as we got into motion, but Miller managed to skid around the corner just in advance of the oncoming avalanche of cross-street traffic. We had a run of three blocks before another signal changed against us, and Miller made a screaming turn to the right, caught an open signal at the next block, turned to the left, and gave it the gas.

Once he had to stop for a closed signal and a stream of traffic pouring against him. The rest of the time it was nonstop.

He pulled up in front of a little apartment house, an unpretentious, two-storied affair only some fifty feet in width, but running the length of a deep lot—the usual type of brick building with a half-hearted attempt made at freshening up the front by the use of white stucco and red tile.

"This is the joint," Miller said.

I handed him a five-dollar bill.

"Want me to wait?"

"No. It won't be necessary."

I consulted the directory. It was all filled up. Most of the cards, however, were slightly soiled. Some of them were printed.

There was no name anywhere on the board which remotely resembled that of Edna Cutler, no card which seemed absolutely fresh.

I pressed the button for the manager. After a while she came to the door.

I gave her my most ingratiating smile. "Two young women who just moved in telephoned me about some automobile insurance. I'm from the Auto Club of Southern California. They wanted to get fixed up with driving licenses and insurance."

"You mean the New Orleans women?"

"Yes."

"Why didn't you ring them? They're in two-seventy-one."

I said, "I'm sorry. I must have had the wrong apartment number. I didn't take down the name, just the number of the apartment. I must have transposed the figures. I had two-seventeen. It didn't answer."

I gave her my best smile while she was thinking that over, and climbed the stairs.

It was dark in the corridor. A ribbon of light was coming from under the door of apartment 271. I closed my fingers over the handle on the door, twisted the knob gently and noiselessly. When I felt the latch had freed, I tried a little pressure.

The door was locked on the inside.

I held the knob in my hand and knocked.

Nothing happened.

I knocked again. There was a sound of motion from behind the door, then shuffling steps, Edna Cutler's voice sounding low and subdued saying, "Who is it, please?"

"Lighting inspector checking up on your wiring installation."

"Well, you can't come in."

I said, "It's a city ordinance. I have to check up on your wiring before you can use the lights."

"Well, we're using them now."

"It'll only take a minute. If I can't inspect them, I'll have to turn them off."

She said, "Come back in an hour," and walked away.

I knocked at the door three times after that, and got no answer.

I looked around the hall and found a fuse box halfway down the corridor; I did a little experimenting, then unscrewed a fuse and put it in my pocket. I went down the corridor. There was no ribbon of light coming out from under the door of 271.

I gently closed my fingers about the doorknob, pushed it in my hand, and held it.

For almost a minute there was silence from the inside of the room; then I heard voices. The voices came nearer to the door.

Edna Cutler said, "Why, that mug! I thought it was just a bluff. I'll bet he *did* shut our lights off."

I heard the sound of a bolt on the other side of the door.

I didn't wait for anything else. I gave the door the shoulder, and felt it strike against something yielding as it came open.

The room was dark, but enough light came in through the open windows from a red neon sign on the corner to bathe objects in a peculiar indistinct ruby-colored illumination.

Edna Cutler had been thrown off balance by the opening door. She was just getting her balance. She had on a pair of shorts and a bra. Back in the far corner of the apartment was another indistinct figure. When I heard her exclamation, I knew that it was Roberta Fenn.

I said to Roberta, "I told you not to get in touch with Edna."

"I—you don't understand, Donald. I *had* to get in touch with her."

Edna Cutler said, "My God, is this that detective again?"

"The same."

"What have you done to our lights?"

"Pulled out the fuse."

"Well, go put it back again."

"And find the door locked when I come back? Nothing doing."

"What do you want?"

I said, "You know what I want. I—"

"What is it?" Edna Cutler asked almost in a whisper as I abruptly ceased speaking.

"Take it easy," I said, quietly. "I was afraid he'd followed you."

There were steps coming down the corridor, slow, steady steps as calmly remorseless as the steps of an executioner approaching the cell of a convict in condemned row.

Edna Cutler said, "I haven't any—"

"Shut up!"

I started for the door, trying to close it. I stumbled over a footstool.

The steps were very near now.

I could hear a slight inequality in them, the walk of a man with a limp.

He reached the door before I did, a man wearing an overcoat with the collar turned up, and a hat with the brim turned down. He didn't seem to be particularly tall, nor particularly thick. The overcoat hid the lines of his figure.

Roberta Fenn screamed.

The man started shooting before I was close enough to do anything about it. One shot at Roberta; then the gun swung toward Edna. By that time I was too close. He knew he couldn't waste that shot. He swung the muzzle of the gun around toward me, and I heard the roar, felt the blast of flame in my face. He missed me, and I was clutching for the hand that held the gun.

I got it.

My old jujitsu lessons came in handy. I whirled so that my back was toward him, holding the wrist, twisting his arm, pulling it over my shoulder. I bent sharply down. The leverage I had gave me everything I needed to throw him over my head and halfway across the room.

There was a commotion in the hallway. Women were screaming. Within the apartment Roberta Fenn was sobbing quietly, and Edna Cutler was swearing.

As the man went over my head, the gun slipped from the nerveless fingers and remained in my hand.

A man's voice in the corridor behind me said, "What's the matter? What's happening?"

I ran past the inert figure on the floor, leaned out the window, and looked down into the pulsing red darkness, illuminated by the neon sign at the corner.

There was more commotion behind me. I heard the sound of a siren a block away.

One of the more venturesome men was coming in the room now.

"What's happening?" he demanded. "What's going on here."

I said over my shoulder, "Someone tried to kill these women. The lights are all off. I think he must have got a fuse in the corridor. See if you can get some lights, will you?"

I leaned farther out of the window and looked up.

There was a brick ledge about three inches wide, running along over the top of the windows. I climbed up on the sill, extended my hand above my head, and gently placed the gun on top of the bricks. Then I slid down and back into the room. A moment later the lights came on.

The man's voice called down the corridor, "Does that fix it?"

I shouted, "Okay, that fixes it."

The man who lay on the floor was sprawled out awkwardly. His soft felt hat lay some six feet beyond the crumpled figure. The arms were outflung, and the skirts of the overcoat had doubled up when he fell so that they were up beneath his head.

The man was Marco Cutler.

CHAPTER TWENTY-THREE

I SAT IN RONDLER'S OFFICE, a bright light illuminating my features. A court stenographer was taking down every word I said. A couple of detectives sat watching me with the intense concentration which one sees on the faces of men around a poker table.

Edna Cutler and Roberta Fenn occupied chairs on one side of the room. Bertha Cool sat opposite them on the other side, and Emory Hale was seated beside Bertha.

Rondler said, "Apparently, Lam, you located Roberta Fenn in Shreveport and brought her with you to Los Angeles."

"Any objection?" I asked.

"The New Orleans police were looking for her."

"They didn't tell me so."

"You knew the newspapers were trying to find out what had happened to her."

207

"I didn't know newspapers were entitled to any priority. I knew her life was in danger. I wanted to give her a break."

"How did you know it was in danger?"

"Because she was mixed up with Edna Cutler, and, between them, if they ever got their heads together, they knew too much."

"You mean about this Craig killing?"

"That and other things."

"Tell me about Craig."

"Cutler had been doing some business in oil properties for Roxberry. Cutler kept everything in his wife's name so that the account showed on the books as Edna P. Cutler, although Edna didn't know anything about it, and Roxberry had never met Edna. A lot of the property that stood in Edna's name was property which Roxberry really owned. It was oil property. Roxberry died. The wildcat wells came in. Because the deals had been highly confidential, there were no papers covering them. Marco simply sat tight. He stood to clear up half a million dollars if he could keep the trust element of the oil properties a secret, and if he could get a divorce decree holding that all of the property that was in Edna Cutler's name had been placed there for convenience, merely so it wouldn't be in his name, that it was in reality his separate property acquired with funds which he had had prior to his marriage."

Sergeant Rondler started slapping the tips of his fingers against the top of the desk. "That part is all more or less obvious," he said.

I said, "The rest of it is just as easy. Craig began to smell a rat. Cutler had gone too far then to back out. He waited until Craig was out with Roberta, masqueraded as the love bandit, jockeyed Craig into a position where he had to put up a fight, and shot him.

"Edna Cutler had a faint suspicion Roberta had some information which might be of help to her. She

208

followed Roberta to New York, missed her, found her in New Orleans, got acquainted with her, also got acquainted with Nostrander. Nostrander gave Edna an ingenious legal recipe for turning the tables on her husband. Edna took it. She kept Roberta in ignorance of what was going on. Cutler walked into the trap. Later on, when Edna sprang it on him, he knew he had to break down Roberta Fenn's testimony and make her admit the whole thing was a conspiracy. If he could do that, he could get a court to hold that Edna was estopped from raising the point that service had not been made on her. That was his only chance."

"Cutler admits that," Rondler said, "but that's all he admits."

I said, "He hired Hale. He thought a New York lawyer could do the gumshoeing better than a Los Angeles lawyer, but he got Hale to hire a Los Angeles detective agency. In the meantime, Hale had located Edna Cutler, then, through Edna, he'd found Roberta. He'd tried to soften Roberta up and had failed, so he turned us loose on the job. He never did get anywhere with Edna Cutler. She simply wasn't making any slips."

"How about these newspaper clippings and the gun?"

"Roberta probably left the newspaper clippings there. Someone else found them and planted the gun."

"Why?"

"Oh, just to make it look good."

Rondler said, "The gun doesn't match up. The bullet which killed Craig wasn't fired through it."

I nodded.

Hale said, "I hope you're not insinuating that *I* planted anything."

I looked at him and said, "You were a babe in the woods. Pretending to fly to New York the night you intended to pull your fast one."

"What do you mean?" he sputtered.

"I don't know what you intended to do with Nostrander. You may have intended to browbeat him, bribe him, or perhaps impersonate a Federal officer. Probably you were going to offer him a bribe. In any event, you wanted an alibi. Nostrander stayed too long in Roberta Fenn's apartment. You followed him there, and couldn't imagine what was holding him, because you knew Roberta wasn't there. About two-twenty in the morning, you knew you didn't dare put off seeing him any longer. You went up to find out what was keeping him."

"I did nothing of the sort," Hale blustered.

I turned to Rondler. "Naturally, he wants to deny it, what with the murder at two-thirty."

"Do you have any proof of all this?" Rondler asked.

I nodded my head toward Roberta Fenn.

Roberta Fenn said, "This man went up to my apartment."

I grinned at Hale.

He said, "That absolutely is not true. It's a case of mistaken identity. I must have a double."

Rondler played tunes with his fingers.

"What happened up there?" he asked me.

"Where?"

"Up in Roberta's Fenn's apartment when Hale went up and saw Nostrander?"

"I don't know. Hale is the only one who knows. You'll have to get him to tell you."

"I tell you I was never up there," Hale said.

Rondler asked Edna, "How did you happen to get in touch with Roberta Fenn?"

"I put an ad in the paper for her."

"In a Los Angeles paper?"

"Yes."

"Why?"

"I thought her life was in danger, and I wanted to protect her."

"Where was she? Where had she been staying here in Los Angeles?"

"I don't know."

Rondler looked at Roberta. "Where were you staying?"

"In a hotel," she said, "but I can't tell you the name of it."

"Do you know where it was?"

"No. It was—I was sort of tight when I went there."

"Did you get tight all alone?"

"No. I was with somebody."

"Who?"

"I don't know. It was a pick-up."

Rondler looked at me and grinned.

I didn't say anything.

"Why did you walk out on the New Orleans cops?" Rondler asked me after a while.

"Because I had work to do."

"What?"

"I wanted to find Roberta Fenn."

"Why?"

"Because I too thought her life might be in danger."

"Why?"

"Because Marco Cutler had got the New Orleans process server thoroughly sold on the idea that he'd actually served the summons on Edna Cutler. Under those circumstances, all he needed to do was to get Roberta Fenn out of the way and it would be the process server's word against Edna's. The court would be pretty apt to take the process server's statement."

Rondler said, "Well, it's a nice theory. The trouble is that we haven't got a damn thing on anybody. Marco Cutler says that *you* are the one who shot at *him*, that he just went up to see his wife, that he never touched the fuse box. He found the door open. You shot at him as he came into the room, then grabbed him in the dark and threw him over your head."

211

"He shot," I said.

"Well," Rondler demanded irritably, "where's the gun?"

"The window was open. It must have gone out of the window in the struggle."

Rondler said, "One of the tenants says you opened the window."

"I went over to the window and looked out. That probably brought on the confusion. You know how excited people get."

Rondler said to Hale, "And I don't suppose you'll admit seeing Nostrander the night he was murdered?"

"Who, me?" Hale asked.

"Who the hell did you think I was talking to?" Rondler asked.

Hale said with dignity, "I was in New York. Look up the records of the airplane passengers."

I grinned at Rondler. "Look up the records of the airplane company, and you'll find that the man who made the trip to New York weighed a hundred and forty-six pounds. Hale weighs about two hundred. Marco Cutler is the lad who answers that description."

"Preposterous!" Hale said. "The records of the airplane company are in error."

I lit a cigarette.

Rondler said, "Well, I guess that's all of it. You folks can go, but don't any of you leave the city without my consent. In a way, you're all in custody as material witnesses, and will be under surveillance."

We all filed out into the corridor. Hale said to Roberta Fenn, "I regret the deception I practiced on you. I got acquainted with Edna Cutler. I couldn't get anything out of her, but I did get her to give me a letter of introduction to you. You'll understand how it is."

"Oh, sure," Roberta Fenn said. "It's all in a lifetime."

I stretched and yawned. "Well, I've had a hard siege of it," I said. "I'm going home and go to bed."

Bertha looked at me with those glittering, intense eyes of hers, said, "Let me talk with you a moment, Donald."

She hooked her arm through mine, drew me off to one side. Her voice was positively motherly. "Now, Donald. You *must* get some sleep. You're all in."

I said, "Certainly. That's why I'm breaking up the party."

She lowered her voice, said out of the side of her mouth, "If you're going to get that gun and try planting it, it's too dangerous. Tell me where it is and *I'll* get it."

"What gun?" I asked.

"Don't be a damn fool," Bertha said. "Do you think I don't know an agency gun when I see it? Where's the other one?"

I said, "In my apartment in the upper dresser drawer."

"Okay. Where do you want it?"

"Just any place. Under Edna's apartment window. Don't leave any tracks."

Bertha said, "Trust me. I think they're shadowing you. Is the gun Cutler used on you out of the way?"

"For a while—I hope. By then I should worry."

Roberta Fenn came walking directly toward us. "May I intrude for just a moment?" she asked.

Bertha said, "It's all right. I'm finished."

Roberta's eyes were caressing me. She gave me both her hands. "Darling!"

CHAPTER TWENTY-FOUR

LIEUTENANT PELLINGHAM came stamping into the office about 12:45 Tuesday. Elsie Brand told me he was out in the other office, and I went out to talk with him.

"I hope you don't hold any hard feelings, Lam."

"I don't if you don't."

"You should have told me you were trying to protect Roberta Fenn because you thought she was in danger."

"Then you'd have taken her into custody and dragged her back to New Orleans."

"Well," he admitted at length, "there may be *something* to that."

"To say nothing of Edna Cutler," I went on.

He said, "Lam, you're rather a deep one. I wish you'd tell me exactly what happened in New Orleans."

"You mean Nostrander?"

"Yes."

I looked at my watch, and said, "I've got an appointment down the street in twelve minutes. It'll take me just about ten minutes to walk there. I'll want to be on time. What do you say we get started? We can talk as we walk."

"All right. I'll appreciate any tip you can give me. My mission out here has been a failure. Louisiana may extradite Roberta Fenn, but I don't think so, not on the evidence available at the present time. If I could go back with a solution of that murder case, it would be a big feather in my cap."

I said, "All right, let's go."

I picked up my hat, walked over to Elsie Brand's desk, and shook hands.

Her face showed surprise. "Going away?" she asked.

"Yes. I may be gone for a while. Take care of yourself."

There was a strange look in her eyes. "You make it sound very final."

"Oh, I'll be back."

We walked out. She followed me with her eyes until the door closed.

Just as we were getting out of the elevator, we met Bertha Cool. Bertha put on her best smile for Pellingham. "Heard the news, Donald?" she asked me.

"What?"

"Sergeant Rondler found the gun Cutler had used where it had been thrown out of the window of Edna Cutler's apartment. A test bullet fired from it showed that *it was the same gun that killed young Craig.* Cutler's yelling frame-up, but they're really going to town with him now, giving him a real third degree."

"That's good."

"Where are *you* two going?" Bertha asked.

"Just down the street a way. Walk along with us. Pellingham said he wanted to talk."

She looked at the elevator as though wondering whether to come along, then said, "We-e-ll, I wanted to go to the office. I've ordered a bunch of genuine silk stockings. I want to see if they've come. Oh, well, I'll walk along, yes."

We walked three abreast down the sidewalk, Bertha on the inside, Pellingham in the middle, while I walked along on the outside.

Pellingham said to me, "You really think Hale went up to that apartment at two-twenty in the morning?"

"I'm sure he did. What have you found out about him?"

He grinned. "He isn't a lawyer at all."

"I didn't think he was. A private detective?"

"Yes. Head of a New York detective agency. Cutler employed him to get some admissions out of Roberta

Fenn, or to get something on her. To tell you the truth, I think *he* planted that whole evidence there in Roberta's New Orleans apartment, hoping he could bring pressure to bear on her by threatening to open up that old murder case and make it appear she was the guilty party. The price of his silence was to be her giving testimony that would make it appear there was a conspiracy between her and Edna Cutler."

"Sounds reasonable," I said.

"Where they fell down," Pellingham went on, "was in not realizing the gun they had dug up somewhere and planted in the desk would eventually be checked to see whether it had fired the murder bullet."

I said, "Of course, if Roberta had caved in and done what they wanted, the gun and the clippings would have been delivered to *her*."

"That's right, yes. I'd never thought of that."

I said, "Perhaps all they wanted was to bring pressure on her."

"There's something to that," Pellingham said. "A lot of it isn't clear as yet—little details. There are some angles on this, however, that I think *you* could clear up."

"Such as what?"

"Giving me a hint on which I could work on Nostrander's murder. *Did* Hale do that?"

I looked at my watch. It was five minutes to one. "I'll tell you something," I said, as we waited for a signal to change. "Bertha Cool and I were the first ones to find that body."

"What!" he exclaimed in surprise.

Bertha said sharply, "Donald!"

I said, "It's all right. They can't touch us. We reported it. *I'm* the one who telephoned the police."

"Let's have the rest of it," Pellingham said as we moved forward with the changing signal.

"We pressed the buzzer of Roberta Fenn's apartment. Somebody answered the signal and buzzed the door open. We got up to where we could look in the apartment. We could see Nostrander's body. I dragged Bertha away because I thought the murderer must have been in the apartment."

Pellingham nodded.

"He wasn't," I said.

"How do you know he wasn't?"

"Because we watched the building. He didn't leave. No one left the building, except a somewhat elderly woman. Then the police came."

Pellingham said, "That's the strange thing about it. After the police got that anonymous tip over the telephone, two detectives went down there. They rang Fenn's apartment, and somebody buzzed the door open. They went up, and there was no one in the apartment."

I said, "The night I went up to call on Roberta Fenn, Nostrander knocked at the door. He hadn't buzzed the outer door. Roberta stalled him along, and then told me I'd better leave. I left right after Nostrander did. When I got out of the street door, I looked up and down the street. I didn't see Nostrander anywhere."

"Well, what's the answer?" Pellingham asked impatiently.

I said, "Nostrander must have had some other friend in the apartment house, a friend on whom he'd been calling pretty regularly. It's pretty reasonable to suppose that this would be a girl friend, and that when she realized that Nostrander was still infatuated with Roberta Fenn she'd be pretty jealous. Marilyn Winton has the apartment right across the hall from Roberta's apartment.

"After the murder, various people came to that apartment house, rang the bell of Roberta Fenn's apartment, and the entrance door was promptly buzzed open. If Roberta Fenn had returned to her apartment, she'd have been killed, but whenever the wrong people entered the apartment, they didn't find anybody there. What every one has overlooked is that *the occupant of any apartment can press the buzzer which opens the street door.* Figure it out for yourself."

Pellingham scowled savagely.

I said, "Marilyn Winton says she heard the sounds of the murder taking place at two-thirty. She's the only one that did. I think if you give Hale the right sort of third degree, you'll find that he was actually talking with Nostrander at about two-thirty. Suppose after he left, Marilyn Winton walked into Roberta Fenn's apartment, looking for a showdown."

"But she heard the sound of a muffled shot at two-thirty."

"She *says* she did. If I intended to go into someone's apartment and kill him at three o'clock, I could manufacture a pretty good alibi by telling my friends that just as I opened the street door of the apartment I'd heard a shot at two-thirty, couldn't I?"

Pellingham kept looking at me as though I'd jerked a veil from in front of his eyes.

Bertha Cool said, "Fry me for an oyster!"

Pellingham gave a low whistle. He reached a sudden decision. "All right, Lam," he said, "you're going back to New Orleans with me."

"That's what *you* think," I told him, and walked up the stairs and through the entrance to the Navy Recruiting Bureau, before either of them knew where I was going.

I said to the man behind the desk. "Donald Lam reporting for duty."

"Okay, sailor. Go through that door. There's a bus waiting out in back. Get in."

Bertha and Pellingham got in each other's way, each trying to get through the door first. Pellingham had forgotten his Southern manners.

A man in uniform stuck a bayonet across in front of them. They stopped as though they'd been figures performing on a picture screen and the film had stopped.

Pellingham pointed his finger at me. "I want that man."

The man behind the desk said, "So does Uncle Sam."

I turned and blew a kiss to Bertha. "I'll send you a postal card from Tokyo," I said, and walked through the back door.

CHAPTER TWENTY-FIVE

I READ ABOUT THE BLOWOFF in the paper as I was approaching San Francisco on a train packed with young Americans who were looking for a scrap.

Hale had told the whole story as soon as he realized he wasn't going to get hooked for murder. He'd been shadowing Nostrander. Everything else had failed. He wanted Nostrander to admit that the service of the papers on the wrong woman was a put-up job. He found Nostrander in Roberta Fenn's apartment, and Nostrander was drunk. Hale had been prepared to offer him a ten-thousand-dollar bribe to sell out, and because he didn't want to get hooked for bribery in case Nostrander refused, he'd built up an elaborate alibi that would make it appear he'd gone to New York by plane.

Marilyn Winton had been placed under arrest. Police had the deadwood on her. She'd been trying to get Nostrander to marry her. That was the unfortunate love affair which had turned her sour on the world.

Marco Cutler had confessed to the murder of Craig, but he still insisted that police had planted the gun. He claimed that he'd actually ditched the murder weapon in New Orleans in an apartment which had formerly been occupied by Roberta Fenn so that his detective, Hale, could bring pressure to bear on Roberta.

As the train pulled into San Jose and stopped for twenty minutes, I sent Bertha Cool a wire:

Edna Cutler should be good for a ten thousand fee because we have brought undisclosed assets into the community funds. Silk stockings aren't made in Japan. Will send you a cherry blossom instead. Love.

The man at the Western Union counted the words, took my money, said, "You'll want to put an address on this, Mr. Lam, where the party can reply?"

I didn't crack a smile. "Care U.S.N., Tokyo," I said. He wrote it down.

>>> If you've enjoyed this book and would like to discover more great vintage crime and thriller titles, as well as the most exciting crime and thriller authors writing today, visit: >>>

The Murder Room
Where Criminal Minds Meet

themurderroom.com